A Novel

ZUNI STEW

Zuni Stew
Chuleya:we

Kent Jacobs

SUNSTONE
PRESS

SANTA FE

Sunstone books may be purchased for educational, business, or sales promotional use.
For information please write: Special Markets Department, Sunstone Press,
P.O. Box 2321, Santa Fe, New Mexico 87504-2321.

Cover artwork by Mario Perez (Bodeguero) and Sallie Ritter
Book design › Vicki Ahl
Body typeface › ITC Benquiat Std
Printed on acid-free paper
∞
eBook 978-1-61139-325-5

Library of Congress Cataloging-in-Publication Data
Jacobs, Kent, 1938-
  Zuni stew : a novel / by Kent Jacobs.
    pages cm
  ISBN 978-1-63293-027-9 (softcover : alk. paper)
  1. Zuni Indians--Medicine--Fiction. 2. Shamans--New Mexico--Fiction. 3. Doc-
tors--New Mexico--Fiction. 4. Indians--Government relations--Fiction. I. Title.
  PS3610.A356438Z66 2014
  813'.6--dc23
                                    2014034388

WWW.SUNSTONEPRESS.COM
SUNSTONE PRESS / POST OFFICE BOX 2321 / SANTA FE, NM 87504-2321 /USA
(505) 988-4418 / ORDERS ONLY (800) 243-5644 / FAX (505) 988-1025

For my Sallie

1973

January 17—After fifteen years of military involvement, the
  Vietnam War ends. The draft is discontinued.

April 4—Tower Number Two of the World Trade Center opens.

April 30—Haldeman and Ehrlichman resign as a result of the
  Watergate scandal.

June 1—Dr. Jack D'Amico completes his internship at Cook
  County Hospital in Chicago.

1

The ER was overwhelmed that night, as usual.

The on-call doc closed the heavy once-white curtain. The patient, a repeat, was going to live. He had treated the same guy for gunshot wounds three weeks earlier. The .22 caliber bullet had missed critical chest structures, but had torn a path through the spongy tissue of the right lung. Tubes in place, the lung cavity drained of pooling blood. A respirator kept the gang member out of acute respiratory distress.

"You again?" said Dr. Jack D'Amico.

"Yeah, man."

"I give up. You're gonna die one of these times. Dumb ass, clean up your act."

The patient's hand moved under the sheet. A square-headed gun barrel pointed at D'Amico's crotch. A Glock. A godamned Glock.

D'Amico pulled a prescription pad out of his lab coat and carefully showed it to his patient. "What do you want? I can write you a scrip to take you to heaven."

Bubbles of blood oozed from the man's lips. Still, he managed to say, "Mercy, me-o-my. Git me the best..." He closed his eyes.

Jack spun, tore open the curtain, yelling, "Code Zero. Code Zero!"

A Chicago cop was on it in a millisecond. Revolver drawn, a truncheon in the other hand. He lunged for the bed, knocking the Glock to the linoleum floor. The patient screamed, tried to pull out tubes, attempted to get out of bed. The cop had him in a chokehold. A male nurse arrived with restraints.

Jack looked in at the controlled chaos. "Better job, George. No holes in the wall this time."

"Doctor D," called a nurse. "Number eight. Hurry, she's crowning."

"A multip?"

"Her ninth."

"A grand multipara. I'm flying." Dodging a cart, squeezing between two gurneys, all Jack could think of was what happened as he observed a young resident trying to deliver a woman with her tenth baby. The baby's head was showing, and the doctor had said something that pissed off the mother. She sat right up, stopped the delivery and demanded another doctor. Whoa—women with multiple deliveries can show amazing control. This delivery went okay. Considering he had only time to pull on sterile gloves.

Stepping out of the delivery room, he saw ER personnel running toward the entrance. Two ambulances, another immediately behind. A tenement fire; victims were being brought to Cook County Hospital as quickly as they could be extracted from the out-of-control inferno.

"Triage!" yelled an intern.

Jack ran the length of the ER, out the swinging doors. Five gurneys were rowed up. Ambulance personnel hovering. The ER resident stood rock-still, like an icicle in a blizzard. How the guy had gotten through med school, let alone grade school, was mind-boggling to the staff. Jack hadn't bothered to remember his name. Covered the dumb doctor's butt too many times. It had gotten so bad, Jack referred to him as 'A.H.'—even to his face.

Jack and two other interns assessed the status of each patient. Twice, he pushed A.H. out of the way to start IVs. Told orderlies to 'haul ass' and get the worst off to ORs.

The ER was expeditiously cleared of burn victims, most shipped to surgical ICU. More patients arrived simultaneously. Knife victim. An elderly man with profound pneumonia. Two car-crash victims. A couple of moribund alcoholics.

A. H. stood over the stabbing victim, holding the man's wrists, watching the second hand on his watch. Jack shoved him aside, yelled for a saline IV, and a lab tech to type and cross-match his blood. At the same time, he tore the man's shirt open. Puncture wound in the left side of the abdomen. He had the victim on his way to the OR in minutes.

The arriving patients were treated as well as a top concierge at a five-star hotel. Jack finally looked at his watch. 7:20 PM. His final shift at Cook County had officially ended two hours and twenty minutes ago. He was no longer an intern. He was a full-fledged DOCTOR.

"It's all yours, A. H.," called Jack, without even glancing back at the ER. Signed out, he headed for the cafeteria. He waved at the girls in their hairnets and grey uniforms, blowing kisses and tapping the glass.

"We'll miss you, honey," called a wizened lady. "Miss you plenty."

"I know, but I gotta go out into the big, bad world. Practice what they taught me, Miss Betty. Pay back my Daddy."

"God be with you, boy. Come back and visit us."

No way, he thought, but said, "You betcha, love to you all."

A last stop at the personnel office where he turned in his ID badge. He decided to walk through the main lobby to say goodbye to the large bronze sculpture of a family amidst a fountain, dubbed 'The Incontinent Family.'

So much for art, for humanity. He hadn't seen much humanity in the last year. Pimps. Poverty. Drugs. Death. He had seen so much pain, injury, loss in that building. He became immune.

He didn't want to be a part of President Nixon's 'Imperial Society.' Medicaid. So-called government-funded healthcare for the poor. Sanctimonious, well-meaning. But will it work in a society that is sick itself?

He crossed West Harrison, headed for the neighborhood bar. 'Ward 17' to the staff. He was running late, no time to celebrate. He dropped some change, picked up a newspaper. Ran for the Medical Center subway. An ambulance screeched around the corner, siren muffled, nearly hitting him. The driver high-fived and headed for the ER.

The subway car emerged from beneath the ground onto the elevated track crossing downtown Chicago. Daylight faded. Transfer to the north shore commuter train. Seat near the door. Dressed in greens, he felt the chill. The air was brisk for summer. A glow emanated from sprawling tract houses, punctuated by neon shopping malls. The lights flickered on. He took out the *Tribune*, went straight to the crossword puzzle. Stumped on the first three clues, he realized he had been on duty for twenty-six hours straight. His brain drained.

The conductor called out, "Next stop, Evanston."

His brother had better still be waiting for him. Winnetka, a world away from Cook County Hospital.

2

Jack awakened at five. (An ingrained habit.) For the first time in a year, he could have slept in. No call, no rounds to make. Disgustingly wide awake, he slipped on old jeans and a T-shirt, patted his hard-sleeping sheepdog, Wooly, and left the guest house.

The Winnetka home was grand. A thirty-foot-tall weathered copper dome above the marble foyer. A walnut table dating back to the Italian Renaissance. Roses, lilies and palm fronds in a silver champagne bucket. Crystal chandelier from Murano. To the right was the formal dining room, a table seating twelve, lined with cream-colored leather chairs. An Italian tapestry rescued from a village hall during World War II hung at one end of the room, a sideboard below, lined with ornate silver crosses. The opposite wall held shelves filled with more silver behind glass doors. A silver domed trolley rested in front.

The library was to the left, reached by a pair of eleven-foot-high doors. Books, of course. Rare port in a locked cabinet. Touches of Rose everywhere: needle-point pillows, candles from a favorite shop in Florence, and because the garden was at its height, more roses in crystal vases.

Jo Lou was on her knees cleaning the oven, but she sat back as he came in the back door. "Doctor Jack, your mother said you'd be sleeping late. I'll fix you some breakfast right fast."

"No problem, Jo Lou," he said, bending down to give her a hug. "Just coffee." He stepped into the hexagonal breakfast room and picked up the *Chicago Tribune*. The paper was strewn about on the bright yellow-enameled round table. He knew his father had already had breakfast, long gone to his office. Jack had been there once when he was just a kid, and that wasn't by invitation. As a growing boy, he was more welcome in the D'Amico Corp construction site trailer, wearing an oversized hardhat, peering over his uncle's drawing table or arm-wrestling with the crew.

Jack's grandfather, Paolo D'Amico, had founded the construction company. At the death of the grandparents, the company had been divided equally between Pasquale and his half-brother, Gabriel. Pasquale, tired of battling with local government rules and regs—and corruption—had sold all but ten percent of his share to Gabriel. With that money, he created the restaurant. It became Pasquale's stage; an elegant club-like atmosphere for the wealthy of the Chicago area to show off their furs and jewels, for CEOs to entertain in private over expensive brandy and cigars.

As he finished the crossword puzzle and began a second cup of coffee, Rose arrived, with Wooly at her side. "You're up early, Jack."

"Yeah." He stood and accepted a kiss on each cheek. A wet-muzzled kiss from Wooly. "The table is new."

"It just arrived. I saw Monet's kitchen in Giverny, yellow and cobalt blue. What do you think?"

Wooly barked, and Jack opened the door to the expansive yard. "When did you and Dad go to France?"

"Spring, of course, to see the flowers. On the spur of the moment—I went by myself." Jack's eyebrows went up questioningly. "You know, Easter and Mother's Day are so busy at the restaurant. He didn't dare leave."

"Then why does he pay his manager so well?"

"You forgot Mother's Day...again."

"I was on call, you knew that. I sent flowers." In the distance, he could see a gardener deadheading roses. Wooly lumbered across the manicured grounds. Hedge clippers in his mouth. "Wooly's getting old; I had to help him up on to my bed."

"Arthritis, his hindquarters. The vet prescribed a supplement." Rose coughed a deep, rattling cough. "He's such a dear dog." She fumbled for a tissue.

"That cough sounds nasty, Mother." He constantly worried about her. She carried herself with such dignity, but she seemed smaller, frailer each time he saw her. Her pale hands rested on top of the newspaper, looking even whiter against the dingy newsprint. Morning light, like the oil washes in Turner's Venetian scenes, streamed into the room, forming a halo-like illusion around her white hair.

Pasquale made certain she saw the finest respiratory doctors in the Chicago area, as well as a yearly assessment at a private clinic in Canada. But with asthma and age betraying her, the prognosis wasn't good. Rose was the tenth member of the Anitoli family to be afflicted with severe asthma. The other nine had died of acute respiratory failure.

"The entire family will be at the restaurant tonight," Rose said, clearing her throat. "Your father has flown in fresh lobster just for you."

When Jack and his brother, Nic, arrived, the guys working valet parking were running to keep up with a steady stream of luxury cars. Mercedes Benz. Rolls Royce. A Lamborghini.

"Whew," said Jack. "This place is hopping."

Almost everyone was already seated in the private dining room. Before Pasquale entered the room, he muttered to his maître d', "That bastard got me again. I donated the champagne, Dom Perignon—his choice. Refused my *proseccos*. Then he twisted my arm to buy three one-thousand-dollar seats to round out a table."

He stopped first behind his wife. Gave her a kiss on her neck. Jack stood and was immediately met with a resounding bear hug from his father.

"What's going on tonight?" Jack asked.

"Private fundraiser for Ravinia." Pasquale signaled all in the room to stand. His voice deep, emotional. *"Voglio fare un brindisi in onore di mio figlio.* A toast to my son." He raised his glass, looking straight at him. *"Jack, io e tua madre ti ringraziamo per averci repagato di tutu i sacrifici che abbiamo fatto per farti studiare."* Laughter filled the room. Pasquale and Rose had every right to chide their son about the cost of his education. Then came the serious stuff. *"Oggi sei dottore con tanto di laurea. Il primo dottore nella famiglia!"*

Jack actually saw tears well up in his father's eyes. He did not expect what came next. *"Grazie, Jack. Salute!"* His father thanked him. Thanked him for becoming a doctor. Amazing.

Italian greetings and congratulations were noisy. Kisses on cheeks, moist eyes.

Only Uncle Gabriel missed the toast. He was late—a last minute dispute with the city forced him to meet with the company attorneys. Some bureaucrat had decided a derrick at a building site was inadequately stabilized. Work was halted until the problem was resolved. His crews were idle. Deadlines loomed, the company threatened with fines.

Jack couldn't remember when he had last set foot in the VIP dining room. Paneled walnut walls, capped by the classic French lip egg-and-dot pattern. Two sandstone friezes, carved by Carl Milles, flanked the doorway. (The stylized eagle heads looked more Germanic than American.) Across the table, his twin sisters were barely visible through an extraordinary bouquet of hybrid teas and floribundas. He would have to look at the rose garden before he left, and told his mother so.

The chandeliers dimmed, the heavy double doors closed for privacy. "So, Doctor D'Amico, what do you think of our new front entrance?" Pasquale said, adjusting his cuff.

"The stairs—you kind of glide up them."

"My exact intention—makes women look like royalty."

"It's in the stringers, the ratio of rise to tread and the total runs," said Gabriel, taking the empty seat at the table. "Not easy to calculate."

"You have draftsmen to do that now," said Pasquale.

"Yes, but I did it myself. Tell me, did you cook for us tonight?" asked Gabriel.

Pasquale laughed. "Touché. I have chefs, but I've done it myself, too."

"And well you did, may I say, very well indeed."

The restaurant was hidden in woods a short distance from the tony northern suburb of Chicago, Lake Forest. His father said he chose the spot to make patrons search for it. Exclusive, discrete, a superb *chef de cuisine* from Tuscany. No wonder reservations ran a month or more ahead. (Thank God for expense accounts).

Liquor flowed, especially Johnny Walker Red. Wine bottles appeared in rows down the table. The chef was at his very best: *cozzes Calabrese*—mussels with Calabrese sausage and faro, preceded Maine lobster, followed by Jack's favorite: *tiramisu.* Rose directed the waiter to bring the gifts to Jack. A silver letter opener engraved with the date of his graduation, from Tristina and Giavanna. A box of stationary, pre-stamped at eight cents a pop, from Rose and Pasquale, and a pre-paid insurance policy on the new car they had given him before the party. A leather briefcase from his brother.

"To carry your money to the bank," said Nic.

Uncle Gabe handed Jack a thick envelope. "He won't be making anything for a while. This will help. I'm so proud of you, Jack." They exchanged a back-thumping hug.

"More wine, anyone?" asked Nic.

Jack nodded, no, then looked at his empty dessert plate, knowing he faced two long years away from food and drink like this. But he wasn't going to Vietnam, like one of his best friends back in 1969. When he had received his orders from the U. S. Public Health Service, Division of Indian Health, he was pretty sure New Mexico was between Texas and Arizona, but he didn't have a clue where to find Zuni.

Pasquale had never heard of Zuni either. When Jack explained that it was an Indian reservation in northwestern New Mexico, quite a discussion had followed, his father doing the conversing. In his opinion, there were only two places in the west worth visiting—Las Vegas and Reno. No argument from Jack, he wasn't happy with the posting either.

The maître d' interrupted, whispering in Mr. D'Amico's ear, who then walked briskly out of the private dining room.

The evening was clearly over.

Rose left in Gabriel's car; Jack and the twins rode with Nic. Rose turned down an after- dinner drink in the library with the men, kissed them all on both cheeks, and slowly walked upstairs with her girls.

Uncle Gabe opted for a glass of port. Nic retrieved the key and unlocked the cabinet for him. Beer and shooters for the brothers. Gabe was in the middle of telling a good dirty joke when the pop of a champagne cork stopped him mid-sentence. Rose and the twins entered, Jo Lou close behind with a silver tray bearing champagne glasses. Rose poured, smiling broadly.

"To my son, with congratulations. Now, drink, sit. Lights out, girls. Jack, they have a surprise for you." Rose swallowed hard, added, "Pasquale can see it later."

As darkness enveloped the room, the twins took turns explaining what they had put together for a class project—Film as Art. Jack knew they had been filming at the hospital, but hadn't paid attention. He should have.

The projector lamp clicked on and the short film began, titled, "A Day in a Young Doctor's Life—36 Hours On—12 Hours Off," directed by Tristina and Giavanna D'Amico. First scenario: 8:00 PM.

The film began with Jack jogging for the elevator, saying between breaths, "Celebrity in 321. He's a rock star, police all over the place. Supposed to sing tonight." The patient was disoriented, on the verge of becoming comatose. An overdose or acute infection looked likely; Jack did a spinal tap, confirmed his diagnosis. The rocker had meningitis.

At 4:00 PM the next day, Jack was seen leaving a private room on the fourth floor. "The senator—heart attack. He wanted his briefcase," Jack said with a smile. "It was big and heavy, important stuff, I thought, he showed it to me—six bottles of Jack Daniels. He asked me for a paper cup."

The third look into his tenure at Cook County showed an exhausted, heavy-lidded Jack racing for the ER early the next morning.

"ER Cubicle A-eight," called a nurse. "Acute abdomen, he's twenty-six. We're waiting for a bed."

Jack went with a diagnosis of peritonitis, and worried about operating—infection was on his mind. He needed tests and a consultation.

The next frame showed Jack sitting on a plastic chair in a semi-dark hallway, head bowed, hands clasped over his head. Tristina's voice could be heard as Giavanna, holding the camera, went for a close-up. Sweat ringed Jack's forehead and green cap at the hairline. A wet curl of hair looked frivolous and out-of-place on his grey-toned skin.

Early the next morning, cursing a hangover, Jack packed quickly in the dark. It didn't take long; he took just a few clothes, knowing he would be in uniform all-too-soon. His stereo, box of classical LP's. He began searching for Wooly. Guessing the big mutt was off prowling or sleeping over at neighbors, he thought better of putting him through the trip. Besides, Rose might need Wooly more than he did.

He trotted down the steps from his room over the garage, drank some milk from the bottle in the kitchen frig, left a note on the breakfast table, and was off. The dark green Thunderbird was a two-door model, gear shift on the console at his side. He merged into the stream of headlights onto US 55. Springfield. St. Louis. Jefferson City, a bit out of his way, but closer to US 54—a straight line to New Mexico.

Fatigue began setting in. His mind drifted back to the family dinner the night before. He had never seen his father react so abruptly, so coldly. Late that night, through a Scotch haze, Nic had mentioned some sort of rumble brewing, something he thought centered on a new federal building in the city center.

Jefferson City, Missouri, time to stop. He pulled into a small motel beside a truck stop, and by the looks of the packed parking lot, he judged the food must be pretty good.

The room was tiny, twin bed, straight-back chair, bedside table. Dinky TV. Wires dangled from the window air conditioner, but he didn't care, all he wanted was a shower. He stepped from his room still a little damp, (cheap threadbare towel), locked the door, and headed across the parking lot toward the flashing green neon café sign. Something made him turn around. The Thunderbird was gone—less than fifteen minutes—dammit, gone!

He sprinted across the lot, around the café and body shop. A new girl was on duty at the motel office. Maybe fifteen, flat-assed dumb. Without asking, he reached over the counter for the telephone and dialed the operator.

Jack's butt was aching from an hour of sitting in a folding chair. The night shift officer accomplished nothing. An 'all-points bulletin' was broadcast statewide. That was it.

After a sleepless night, he finally located a used Chevy which he could afford—thanks to Gabe. Since his two duffle bags were in the Thunderbird's trunk, he walked the three miles to the dealership with only his Dopp kit in hand. On US 54 by noon.

3

The 1955 faded salmon and white Chevrolet crossed the Osage. The radio didn't work. By the time he crossed into Kansas and stopped for gas in Fort Scott, he felt the humidity sucking out his energy. Gas was sixty-seven cents per gallon, two cents higher than Chicago. So much for middle-American values.

His T-shirt clung to his chest, perspiration burned his eyes. He pulled off the soaked shirt, wiped the sweat from his face, dropped some change in the red Coca Cola machine. He bartered (not very long) with the young cashier for a large cup of ice. It didn't take long to get her to offer him a second.

He felt her watching him as he propped the bottles and ice in the passenger seat. She appeared beside him, offering a wax-paper-wrapped ham sandwich.

The oscillating heat waves rising from the pavement reminded him of how his mother suffered during the Chicago summers. Pasquale oversaw the construction of a lakeside summer home in northern Minnesota for Rose and the kids.

He opened the sandwich, paying little attention to the near-empty road stretching ahead, then touched the ice-filled cup against his brow. The white bread stuck to the top of his mouth—all-American Rainbow brand. What do they eat on the reservation?

4

Jo Lou started the coffee. While setting the table, she saw the note from Jack. It wasn't folded so she read it: *I'm no good at goodbyes—time for me to face the music and get going. Again, thanks for the great car and dinner. Will call when I reach Albuquerque. Ciao & love to each one of you, Jack.*

By 6:30, Pasquale and Rose sat at the table, drinking coffee, reading and re-reading the note. Jack was the adventurous kid who climbed up on to the table and jumped off. Older brother Nic climbed up, but went down via the chair. The twin girls, both at Northwestern, were another problem. If Tristina painted her nails black, Giovanna would dye her hair pink. They were skinny. Identical Twiggys in mini-skirts.

"Ready for breakfast?" asked Rose, tightening her silk robe. Jo Lou heard her speak and reached in the oven for the platter of scrambled eggs and bacon.

No one heard the two men enter through the service room. A large man in a white button-down shirt crossed the kitchen in two steps, wrapped his hand across Jo Lou's mouth, and using a thin-bladed Norwegian fish knife, sliced her throat. At first she felt nothing, but then a violent searing pain consumed her. Immediately, she felt warm, sticky blood flowing down her chest. That was her last sensation. The assassin silently lowered her to the floor as the second man sidestepped the body. He was the smaller of the two, well-dressed and equally agile.

Unaware, Rose sat with her back to the door, head down, searching for her slippers. Her husband glanced up with a start as the man grunted, "Watch, Pasquale. I want you to see this." He locked an arm around Rose's neck, and drove an eight-inch, large-bore trocar into the left side of her chest, burying it through her rib cage and into her heart. A pulsating spray of blood projected from the hollow, three-sided surgical instrument, striking Pasquale. In moments Rose was dead, her face blue-white, drained of blood.

Pasquale, paralyzed from shock, screamed, "You sonofabitch! You!"

The bodyguard grabbed D'Amico from behind in a vice hold. The other man jerked out the trocar, bent over to wipe it on her delicate robe, then spun around, forcing the trocar up one of Pasquale's nostrils. The tip embedded in the center of his brain.

Pasquale's eyes bulged, lightning sensations burst throughout his body. He gasped for air, for a voice to scream. No air, no sound came forth. His dead weight sagged in the arms of the bodyguard, who released his grip, letting the body thud to the floor.

"The kids now. All of them. Give me the knife, Mario."

Upstairs, they entered each room and, without hesitating, sliced the throats of both Tristina and Giavanna. Blood splattered a bulletin board above the lamp between the twin beds. Two gold chains, each with a crucifix, were draped over the board. A purple pennant emblazoned with the words 'Northwestern Rocks,' was pinned next to a photo of Jack and Nic. The brothers were behind the wheel of a mahogany speedboat, a restored 1940's Chris Torpedo-back.

The man in the suit touched the knife blade to the boys in the photograph and murmured, "Next." The bodyguard followed him down the hall to the end bedroom. Quietly opening the door, they saw Nic sleeping soundly, an empty bottle of Heineken propped by his side. The old sheepdog sprawled across the other twin bed. Nic barely roused as the man silently slid the fish knife across his throat. Wooly stirred, responding mainly to the smell of blood. As the bodyguard stepped between the beds, Wooly wagged his tail and tried to stand. The tan-suited man rolled him over and deftly made a long incision in the dog's soft belly, killing him instantly.

"Boss," whispered the bodyguard. "One left—the doctor."

They knew there was an apartment above the triple garage. The kid, the privileged one, had to be there. The door wasn't locked, the bed slept in but empty, bathroom as well. He touched the sheets—they were cold.

The two men systematically checked the estate. Garages, storerooms, greenhouse, tennis court, pool cabana. The boss checked his suit for bloodstains as they drove away. He wasn't finished. Mario had killed the maid. He himself had killed all of the others—all the D'Amicos, except one.

5

Jack's plan was to stay in Liberal, Kansas, the second night, but he decided to stay in Pratt, Nebraska, some one-hundred-twenty-five miles short of his destination. Ten-plus hours of driving rolled past. In the town of maybe six-thousand, there weren't many choices for motels, so he decided on the one with a diner directly across the street. A shower, then a plate of greasy chicken-fried steak. A buck-ninety.

The lawyer called Gabriel early to report on the compromise. Mixed news. Costly construction, but doable. Gabe wanted to tell Pasquale himself. He turned his white truck into the circular drive, grabbed the plans. After three rings, he jogged around clipped euonymus hedges to the back door. As usual, unlocked. He called out a bright "Good morning" just before entering the kitchen.

He tripped over Jo Lou's contorted legs, knocking him to his knees. His hands went out to stop his fall. The blood was slick, still wet. The breakfast room—the bodies of Rose and Pasquale were on the floor. Pasquale, blood-soaked. Oddly Rose seemed free of blood except for a large spot on the left side of her robe.

Snapping to, he grabbed the phone. The operator repeatedly had to coax him to get the address.

Gabriel waited on the front steps, head down, until the police arrived. Later, in the kitchen, he took a seat facing away from the carnage. He placed nitroglycerin under his tongue. He felt himself ease a little, out of danger.

The senior officer stepped outside to call his superior, who asked him to repeat the surname again. "D'Amico. All of them, and their maid." He was told to sit tight, wait for his return call. Do nothing.

"Do nothing?" he whispered to himself. "What the fuck is going on?"

Unmarked cars arrived. No one commented about the distribution of blood, the bodies upstairs. The chief was emphatic: shut up and leave. A plainclothes team arrived as the policemen drove away.

At one o'clock, Pasquale D'Amico's manager assembled the staff and told them about the departure of the D'Amico family due to Mrs. D'Amico's asthma. Mr. D'Amico was flying her to the specialist in Canada. The daughters and eldest son went with them. Mrs. D'Amico's local physician had phoned him. All was under control. The restaurant would continue business as usual.

◈ ◈ ◈

A large estate in Flossmoor, prestigious-looking, even in this neighborhood. Two men sat on a brick terrace looking down on the pool below. Three young children splashed and shrieked.

Mr. K spoke in a very low voice, "You come recommended. Your target is serving his tour of duty not in Vietnam, but as a doctor at some godforsaken place, New Mexico or Arizona, maybe Utah. As a doc, he couldn't opt out. He's driving a dark green Thunderbird, black Landau roof, really hot shit, that his daddy gave him."

Ice cubes clinked against crystal. Mr. K poured a quarter glass of Scotch for himself, leaned back in his lounge chair. "Can't blame him. I gave that kid's mother—my only child—anything she wanted at that age. Now she's on her second husband. Spends all her time deep sea fishing in Mexico."

"Which coast?" asked the guest.

"West. Last I heard, San Carlos."

"I've been in Guaymas. The *Cabrillo* are huge."

"Bottom fish. I don't like trolling," said Mr. K.

A beach ball headed into a rose bed. The little girl cried as she watched it deflate. Mr. K ignored his granddaughter, studying the man across the glass-topped table.

The forty-ish Mario Bella was stocky, but in prime physical shape. A meticulous man, his hands were not those of a day laborer, but someone you would meet at the country club and play a round of golf. Heavy dark eyebrows, a family trait, and curly salt-and-pepper hair.

"Most likely route he's taking is US 54. Here's his picture, and your new ID." Mr. K reached in the pocket of his thick white terry-cloth robe, slid a driver's license and a set of keys across the table toward him. "The keys go to a Chevy Impala. Find Doctor Jack D'Amico and kill him."

6

It was after midnight when Mario first spotted the dull light emanating from Fort Scott. He realized he had been driving on mental auto mode for some time. A moonless night, an empty road had done nothing to hold his attention. He passed a city limits sign, a sign as uninteresting as all the others on his route.

A car roared out of a small drive-in, fishtailing on to the main drag, barely missing him. "Sonofabitch!" yelled Mario. It was a fancy T-bird. Illinois plates. He floored the gas pedal. The cars were butt-to-bumper.

The Thunderbird swerved off US 54. Mario accelerated out of a slide, ramming the car. Over-correcting, the car shot off the road, down an embankment into thick brush. Upside down, wheels spinning.

Mario slid down the sandy hillside. The kid struggled to get out. Mario raised his pistol and fired. He dragged the lifeless body from the T-bird into the headlights.

It wasn't Dr. D'Amico. "Shit!"

A teenager, with acne and bad teeth. A steel bullet through the upper torso. He kicked the body over with his foot—a clean exit out the boy's back. He dug out the bullet buried in the leather-covered console. Shoved the kid into the car, pushed his dead body into the steering wheel. Saturated him with gas. One lit match, a huge explosion of flames.

Mario ran up the embankment and floorboarded the Impala. Wheels spun in the dirt, the car jumped forward kicking up a plume of dust. An explosion rocked the car. Red fireball lit the sky. He glanced in the rear view mirror. Once.

Back in town, he waited in the bay of a darkened filling station. The Union 76 man opened at five AM, filled his tank while he went into the filthy bathroom. Shaved and brushed his teeth. The water was dirty brown. No paper towels. No toilet paper.

He asked the gas guy, who appeared to be half-asleep, where he could buy a used car.

The man yawned. "There's 'Jerry's' just down the way a bit. Can't miss it. Chain-link fenced lot with a trailer in front."

Jerry wasn't there, but a man who called himself 'the main man' turned out to be about as smart as a stone. He remembered selling an old clunker, a '56 pink Chevy, the day before.

"Guy didn't know nothin' 'bout cars. Hope he makes it where he's goin'."

Jack left in darkness, stopping only to let the engine cool enough so he could add water. The car was using nearly as much oil as gasoline.

Dalhart. Another late night, a lousy motel room. At least the TV worked. The next morning, scorched pancakes and undercooked bacon. The only bright spot—a large cream and pink rose floating in a low vase at the cashier's desk.

"Chicago Peace?" asked Jack.

"You know roses?" smiled the older woman.

"My Mother does."

7

"*C*an't you get a damn thing right?"

"Mr. K..." Mario had to give him some good news or he'd end up eviscerated like that dog. He told him he had found the Thunderbird, but D'Amico must have bought another car, possibly an old Chevy in bad condition.

"Then get going, catch him!" Mr. K slammed down the receiver and paced the walnut-paneled office. At least he had been correct about US 54.

Mario crossed Kansas in a few hours. Two speeding tickets were disposed of out the window. He hated Kansas. He hated driving. He despised Mr. K—worst contract he'd ever been stupid enough to accept. He slammed a tape into the deck—*Götterdämmerung*. Mr. K, a Jew, hated German music, especially Wagner.

An hour later he spotted a pink-toned Chevrolet. Right year, wrong plate. If the stone head in Fort Scott was correct. He unfolded the map, tracing US 54. Get through Dalhart, give up for the night in Tucumcari. Shower, sleep.

About forty minutes out of Dalhart, a loud clang emitted from the right front wheel. Jack barely got the car off the road. He could deliver a baby blindfolded, take out an appendix in the dark, but he didn't know a thing about cars. Something was damn sure wrong.

Twenty more minutes went by before a trucker stopped and offered help. No luck, but the driver radioed for a tow truck, and three hours later he was back in Dalhart, chucking out more dollars for the tow. The mechanic had a cold. He wiped his nose with a greasy rag, promised a look, but nothing more. Wheel studs were sheared off. An anchor pin needed re-welding. Plus a re-attachment of the return spring.

Hours later, he coaxed the car back on to the highway. Ahead, a Greyhound bus spewed fumes. A Harley with bulging saddlebags roared past. A 1957 red Corvette pulled into a motel named Chief's. Black and white shields pointed the way to US 66.

Welcome to Santa Rosa—City of Natural Lakes. Neon at the Frontier Motel flashed:

WELCOME
7 ROOMS
CHEAP CLEAN SLEEP
THERMOSTAT HEATING

He gave up for the day. Pulled in at a place called the Club Café. The iconic logo featured the smiling, satisfied face of the Fat Man. "Greeting Diners Since 1935." Decent T-bone steak and fries.

He decided to dump the Chevy. Too damn slow. Still one-hundred-fifty miles to Albuquerque.

Backing out of the motel parking lot, Mario spotted a pink Chevrolet crammed in a junk yard fifty feet away. Five dollars to check the license plate. Kansas. Another fiver confirmed the driver had sold it for next to nothing and walked away.

There was one used car place in town—McCarthy's. A blue-eyed, young man had purchased a 1961 M151 Willy Jeep an hour before.

Thanks to President Eisenhower and the Highway Act of 1956, US 66 had been newly upgraded to I-40 outside of Santa Rosa, but he ran into a nightmare of road construction by the time he reached Moriarty. Diverted to old 66. Plodded through the blighted town. Mainly truck stops. Hippies and stash houses. He swore he could smell marihuana.

Back on recently built I-40, he began the climb to about seven-thousand-feet through Tijeras Canyon. Winding road. Thunderheads grew vertically over South Sandia Peak. Clouds raced to merge, but occasional flashes of sun lit up granite walls and embedded pink feldspar crystals. The Western Range, steep, rugged towers. He crowned out. A majestic view opened up. The whole world spread out before him. In the distance lay the old town of Albuquerque.

A stiff wind current blew down his back, smelling of ozone. He coasted into the city—a downshift, cruising Central Avenue. The first drops hit the window screen. Nob Hill. Neon signs everywhere. He spotted a new-looking motel, his eyes on the swimming pool, despite the imminent downpour.

Mario stopped in Moriarty. Got gas at the Whiting Brothers Station. Checked into the Sunset Motel. He went out, ate a green chile cheeseburger at the Frontier Bar, which gave him indigestion. He watched TV on a snowy screen in his room. Rhythmic flashing neon lights outside brought on a tension headache.

8

Admiral Zeller cradled the receiver and leaned back, eyes on Dr. G. H. Martin. "That call was from the Chicago FBI."

"What do they want from us?"

"The new officer you're meeting, Doctor Jack D'Amico—his family was murdered in their home a few days ago." Zeller opened a silver box topped with a large chunk of turquoise, a gift from his wife, and offered a cigarette to Dr. Martin.

"His entire family?"

Zeller exhaled, looked at the notes he had taken. "Husband, age sixty-two, and wife, fifty-eight, Jack's father and mother. Twin girls, nineteen-years-old, a son, twenty-eight, the maid, age thirty-three, and a dog, an old sheepdog. Everyone, except Jack, the new doctor."

"My Lord. What are we supposed to do? What can we do for him?" asked Martin.

"The FBI wants us to tell him nothing for now, just get him on his way." Zeller tapped an ashtray. "They need time to sort things out. Meantime, they asked us to protect the guy. They didn't say 'what' to protect him from."

The silence in the office was interrupted only by Zeller opening and closing his lighter. Martin had trouble not looking at the photograph of Zeller's youngest son resting on the credenza behind his boss's desk. Killed in Vietnam. Flying low reconnaissance over the jungle, the boy didn't make it to an age to legally purchase a beer. The admiral still wore a black ribbon on his upper right lapel.

Zeller put the lighter down and gave it a spin. "Make his visit short. Call Doctor Newman, fill him in, then get D'Amico to Zuni. At least it's remote."

◈ ◈ ◈

Jack dried off after an early swim, settled into a lounge chair. Thumbed through the Public Health Service manual. He tossed it on the glass-topped table just as a pretty Hispanic girl set down a breakfast tray.

Between bites of scrambled eggs, he memorized the officer names he was about to face.

Back in his room, he remembered his promise to call home. No need to mention the Thunderbird. He leaned over and snapped on a low lamp. The red-gold-clad bullfighter in the velvet painting went neon. Even the bull's eyes flashed red.

Fourteen rings and no answer. Probably Jo Lou and his mother were in the rose garden, or shopping—it was ten o'clock in Chicago. He would call from Zuni.

He parked adjacent to a 50's-looking concrete block building. Alone in the elevator, the brass fittings and wood panels shined. No hospital smells, no muffled screams, no rounds, no demands—he was completely alone. Everything was totally foreign, his future a blank.

Ushered down a hall to a door marked with the engraved name of Dr. G. H. Martin, Assistant Director. He ran his hands down his sideburns, checked his zipper.

A grey-haired man in short sleeves, tie tack too high, offered a chair. "Welcome to the Southwest, Doctor. We've been expecting you. We're really short-handed out there at Zuni."

That was the first familiar thing Jack had seen or heard: Cook County Hospital was perpetually short-handed.

Martin explained that the Indian Health Service operated in a quasi-military fashion. Rarely would he be on a military base. He was not expected to maintain military etiquette. It was hard for Martin to look into the young doctor's clear blue eyes, knowing of the killings. He tried to hide his empathy. A hollow grew in the pit of his stomach. Luckily, the intercom buzzed, a secretary's voice told them the admiral was expecting them.

As they entered, Mark Zeller stood—six-foot, four-inches—and shook Jack's hand. "Welcome to the service, Doctor. First time out west?" Jack nodded. "What do you think of it so far?"

"I had some great *chiles rellenos* last night at La Placita in Old Town. And my first *sopapillas*."

"You speak Spanish?"

"Poorly, about as good as my high school Latin."

"Make sure you read this," Zeller said, handing Jack a booklet. "From Indian Affairs. Wise advice. In Indian Country, you have to partner with the tribal police and the FBI. They have the trust and respect. They can open doors, especially for us in the Indian Health Service.

"You're going to see and have to report cases of suspected abuse and provide services to the victims. As outsiders we have a certain objectivity and reputation for fairness. To us, it doesn't matter who is what tribe or clan. We just want to provide the best health care."

The meeting over, Zeller said uniforms were at the BX. "Then straight to Zuni?"

"Yes, sir. Already checked out of the motel."

"Good."

Then the admiral did something Jack would later recall as unusual. Zeller reached out to shake his hand, and soundly clapped the other hand on his shoulder. The pressure was firm and seemed to last a bit long, considering he had just met the man, not to mention Zeller far, far outranked him.

"The Zunis are a beautiful people. Handsome. A bone structure that is unique. Not Asian, not flat—no ovoid eyes. Kind of dignified. You will like them. You will find, well, for want of the right word, a level of solace in their world. Godspeed, son," said Zeller.

One hour later, Jack-the-civilian became Jack-the-Navy-Lieutenant-equivalent, shiny double bars on his lapel. All khaki—slacks, short sleeve shirt, socks—all very beige.

He wrestled with the ragtop before leaving Albuquerque. The canvas was bleached, splotchy, threadbare along the seams, but in one piece.

He departed the city on Central Avenue, crossed the Rio Grande, began the climb up Nine-Mile Hill. The land opened up. The narrow two-lane 66 was bordered by desert grassland, barb-wired fences, solitary rows of telephone lines. The sky was huge.

Crossed the Rio Puerco through a truss steel arch bridge. A sign told him he was entering tribal land. Route 66 was stepping back in time. Laguna Pueblo. He regained control of his thoughts; his usual keen sense of observation and assessment returned. His physician's mind, trained to notice any and all nuances, thought back to the brief conversation with the admiral. A distinct sense of urgency. Even sincerity. Everything in place, down to the marked map now on the passenger seat. Strange. Zuni must be very, very short-handed.

The patched highway climbed in altitude, switch-backing, not a person or another car in sight. Static drifted in and out over the radio. He pushed the off button.

Silence.

An empty road, with a turn south to Zuni ahead– piece of cake, he thought. He was smack in the middle of Laguna Indian country, surrounded by flat mesas topped with gradations of indigo, blue-black, then burnt sienna and yellow ochre, a rainbow of earth tones. Rugged buttes striated with shades of lavender were dotted with piñon, which met chalk-colored rock at the base. Wicked. Freakin' awesome.

The route circled around massive wind-carved red rocks. Red-stained arroyos, rich with clay, broke through yellow gramma grass, pockmarked with lava. Lots of volcanic activity in the past. The road opened up, but he was slowed down by a dirt-spattered Ford pickup. A brown arm signaled a turn and the old rusted truck pulled off on a dirt driveway. A corn patch, a horse, and a couple of sheep.

His ears popped. The ecology was changing. A zone of juniper. A mix of piñon and oak. A thicker cover of blue gramma grass. Prickly pears—a first for him. And something else had changed. Eastern New Mexico was ranching country. John Wayne. Leaving Albuquerque, he began to feel the heartbeat of the Spanish and Indian Territory. Everything was old, seasoned with the passing of time. Generations before. Human drama. He felt something he had never experienced before. A sense of mystique. An inexplicable aura.

Thankfully the Jeep was running smoothly, and he planned to tell his father just that—his car was great. The robbery bit could come later. For some reason, he thought of Wooly and wished he could reach across the floor gearshift to pet the old dog. Wooly was almost sixteen, arthritic and partially blind, and not a single person in his family could face euthanizing him. God certainly got the canine life span wrong.

A smile crossed his face, even though his next thought wasn't really all that funny. He could picture the day at the boat house in technicolor. Wooly was just a puppy, he and Nic were little boys, all waiting for their mother and the gardener to take them out in the boat. Somehow Wooly managed to climb onto the roof of the boat house, spotted the boys waving to Rose, and jumped from the roof in obvious glee, crashing straight into frigid water. The silly dog would have drowned if Nic hadn't jumped in to save him. Jack could smell the sunburned days. Med school had distanced him from Nic. Now, he had left him behind again.

He stopped for gas at a Texaco station in Grants, not knowing what would be available at the pueblo. A single lone pump. A bowlegged man appeared at the door carrying a case of empty Coke bottles. A Woolworth bag blew across the cracked pavement and down the empty street. Jack asked him about a place to eat. The man gestured across the street in the direction of bright turquoise cinderblock building.

Wooden booths, plastic-covered menu tacked to the wall. Pretty much Mexican food and burgers, so he went with the Hatch green chile cheeseburger with a side of frijoles.

An older Hispanic man said, *"Bueno. Y* iced tea?" Someone in the kitchen turned up a radio tuned to a Mexican station.

"Si, por favor." He unfolded the Indian Affairs pamphlet he had stuffed in his back pocket. The first sentence read: *Do not speak Spanish on the Zuni reservation!* Strange, he thought, but it became clear as he read on:

Zuni was officially annexed to the Spanish Empire in 1540. For more than a century Spanish friars labored to convert the Zunis to Catholicism, often using brutal techniques. Zuni parents were forced to hide their children from the Spaniards by placing them in windowless grain storage chambers built into cliff dwellings. In many instances, the parents were captured or killed, and subsequently the children perished, their skeletons to be discovered years later by archeologists.

Other pueblos shared religious rituals, and even occasionally intermixing words from their respective languages. The Zunis refused, maintaining their own particular language and culture, and remaining in a single tight-knit pueblo. Zunis ignored the Spanish culture, set aside Catholicism. Even during the Pueblo Revolt of 1680, Zuni played only a small part, choosing to remain in what they believe to be the Center of the Middle Earth.

To this day, Zunis do not believe in intermingling with the outside world except for commerce.

Jack closed the booklet, ate the last of the burger, and was back on Route 66 and across the continental divide, watching for Highway 602. After the turn south, the narrow road dipped and curved through hilly, up-and-down arroyos. A little ribbon of a road, no fences, surrounded by open range, narrowed into a tunnel-like draw of burnt sienna and cream-striped rock.

The single-track road turned sharply left. A blind curve. He hit the brakes, the Jeep grabbed. A goddamned herd of bleating sheep blocked the road. Creeping forward in low gear, peering over their dusty backs, he could barely make out the outline of a truck on the other side of the road, upside down, wheels still turning.

He pulled the Jeep off the road and flung the door open wide. Dodging and jumping sheep, he ran to the truck. An arm dangled out of the window, twisted. Fingers twitched involuntarily. One look inside at the contorted body in the cab. "My God," he said aloud. The arm was nearly torn from the torso just above the elbow. Blood spurted from severed arteries.

He jerked off his shirt and in one swift motion ripped a strip of fabric, wrapped the mutilated stub and formed a tight tourniquet above the elbow, stopping the bleeding. Gasoline. Unable to pry the door open, he reached in and grabbed the young man's shoulders and pulled the torso out the window, dragging him a safe distance away.

The kid was breathing heavily. His eyes opened wide as Jack gingerly probed for other injuries. Ear to his chest. Lungs clear, no gurgling, no broken ribs. He carried him to the back of the Jeep, pushed the plastic bag of new clothes under his legs to keep blood flowing to his brain. He positioned the nearly severed arm on the boy's chest. The kid was conscious, but silent.

At the outskirts of Gallup, he roared through a just-turned-red light. A cop hit his red lights and siren. Jack edged the Jeep off the pavement and waved the cop forward. Once parallel, he yelled, "I'm a doctor. Emergency! He's bleeding out. Lead me to the PHS hospital."

Immediate surgery. Jack and the policeman met up at the admission desk. Surprisingly, the officer could complete most of the forms.

Name: Tito Jahata.

Residence: Zuni Pueblo.

Father: Louis Paul Jahata.

The remaining data was obtained from Tito's driver's license. Jack asked for a lab coat to cover his bare chest.

"You did good, Doc. Very good." The officer added, "Tito is the son of one of the pueblo's most revered *A:shiwani.*"

"What?"

"Rain priest. Responsible for the welfare of total Zuni world," said the officer. "He can do miracles. I have seen."

9

*D*octor's lounge. An hour passed before the senior surgeon showed up. "He's going to be all right. The mutilated arm, no hope, only a useless extremity."

"Could I have done more?"

"You did what was needed, you kept him alive." The surgeon never offered his name.

Jack walked down the green-tiled hallway out to the Willy, ignoring the blood stains in the back. State 602 again, south. The countryside spread before him. Deep cobalt blue sky, dotted with innocent flat-bottomed clouds. Ponderosas towered over patches of mullein, tall grass and chamisa filled the ravines of the rugged hillsides.

West on State 53 in about a half hour. Zuni Pueblo, ten miles down the road.

Just as he reached the last rung on the ladder, he heard the phone ringing. He swung his body through to the roof and headed through the open doorway. His broad-rimmed black hat skimmed the door frame. After hanging up the phone, Louis Paul Jahata took off his hat and dark glasses and walked silently into his cool workroom. The conversation terse, no emotion in the voice of the Zuni woman working at the Gallup hospital. Tito, his son, was alive. A good boy, non-drinker. A candidate to someday become one of the tribal priests or *A:shiwani*. In an instant the spirit world had ended Tito's dreams of becoming an Air Force pilot.

Jahata's mind grappled with the scant facts he had just received—a white man, a doctor, saved him. He listened to the wind.

The breeze fluttered a line of clothes outside his home in the pueblo. A modest home, like all the others. Sepia adobe walls colored by layers of fine sand-based mud, floors the same. In a tiny closet-like space off the sparsely furnished front room, his work bench sat in front of the only window. Buckskin pouches filled with stones, some with silver conchos, were piled to one side. Bundles of dried mountain tobacco hung from a nail. Medicinal herbs hung from a viga above. A shelf contained a row of bear fetishes. His wife of twenty-five-years belonged to the bear clan. Like all Native American men, he joined his wife's clan. The small carvings made from antlers, shell, turquoise or coral would fit in the palm of his hand.

He reached for a fetish, the most primitive, carved by nature with only a minimum of human intrusion, strengthened the bear shape. An arrowhead bound to its back by a fine leather thong gave it strength. The critical insertion of a red coral heartline added great power.

Louis Paul smoothed back his long black hair. A premature white streak ran on the right side of his crown. He wore a tan leather vest over a collarless denim shirt. Worn jeans, silver belt buckle. Scuffed boots. A large pale turquoise ring. Settled on a goatskin, he raised the fetish to his lips and breathed in, inhaling the spirit. As he settled into a trance, he imagined a silver strand extending from each corner of the room to his solar plexus. He prayed silently, using the fetish as a messenger to the spirits that could intermediate to help a humble human.

The prayer began: "Thou art stout of heart and strong of will..."

Bordering marshes at the edge of a lake, Jack passed a cluster of buildings on the right. Three miles further, at the outskirts of the pueblo, he spotted children playing in a dreary stream strewn with bottles, cans, and empty Budweiser cases. He stopped beside the single gas pump at a general store. Flies buzzed over a puddle, a yellow dog strained against a tethered chain. He wagged his tail. Stirred up dust. He opened the screen door and tentatively stepped inside the rock building. Several older men stood huddled at one side of the store, smoking, talking in low voices. The place smelled strongly of mothballs and piñon smoke.

He walked across the creaky floorboards past a black potbelly stove in the center of the room over to an old wood and glass counter. The cases weren't heavily stocked, nor were the shelves above. A few cans of lard, Spam, corn, hominy, salt. A hand-painted sign read: BUY. SELL. TRADE. LIVESTOCK. PAWN. It was obvious that despite all the natural beauty of the reservation, the lack of jobs kept the Zunis in a state of poverty.

Jack's mother, an aristocrat by birth, had immigrated with her new husband to the United States before WWII. Nic, her first-born, was conceived in Italy but born in America. Despite her pedigree, Rose knew all about rationing and poverty during the war in northern Italy. Especially Piedmont, the family estates.

Her younger brother, Danielle, was a member of the Resistance. Formerly an officer in the Italian Army, he refused to join Mussolini's 'Republican' army. A long-time anti-Fascist, Danielle learned the hazards of guerilla warfare: hit and run attacks from alpine hideouts, constant fear and hunger in the severe winters of 1943-45.

Jack read the letters: hunger governed all. Forced to live like animals. Only food mattered. Food for the children. Food for his wife. Food for himself. Food at the cost of depravity and human debasement. Could this be happening here? In the United States? What the hell happened to Johnson's war against poverty?

A grey-haired man with a long ponytail approached. Weathered skin, deeply tanned. Only the skin exposed by his unbuttoned collar was pale by comparison. He wore a plain two-inch-wide silver bracelet on his wrist. No attempt to greet Jack, nor did his rheumy eyes blink.

Finally Jack said, "Could you tell me how to get to your hospital?"

"Three miles back, at Black Rock, by the lake."

Outside, in the blinding sun, Jack looked at the trickling stream and the pollution. The Zunis have us white doctors segregated, he thought, miles from the pueblo.

10

*F*our-thirty. He parked in front of a rock building bearing a small sign: *U. S. Department of Indian Affairs.* He spotted a windsock a short distance away, and suspected an airstrip must be nearby. The sock was limp, the dirt streets empty. A dark stone building at the center of the square turned out to be the U. S. Public Health Hospital, but it looked deserted, definitely not a hotbed of activity. Why the rush-rush in Albuquerque?

Houses encircled the plaza, adobes or rock, in general, a tacky hodgepodge. Jack parked the Willy in front of a pink adobe and walked back to a newer-looking home where he had seen an Indian woman standing outside. As he got closer to her he realized that the grass in front of the house was strewn with dirty dishes.

She wore a long pleated purple skirt, a denim jacket with a corduroy collar and a pork pie hat, and was holding a garden hose. She looked up and said, "Too nice to work inside."

He introduced himself. Continuing to blast the dishes with freezing water, she replied, "I work for the top doc. This his house."

And those were his dishes.

There were no patients in the waiting room. A nurse, a pretty, young Native American wearing a white cap was on the phone, speaking in her native tongue. He waited, taking in the blue-grey walls, peeling trim, the yellowed wax on linoleum floors. He was familiar with the antiseptic smell, but the place also smelled of Pine Sol. The florescent lights blinked, then buzzed, aggravating the tinnitus in his ears. He shut his eyes for a full minute.

A clipboard hit the countertop. "Can I help you?"

"Doctor D'Amico reporting."

"You're late. Follow me." She escorted him down a hall to an office crammed with three government-issue grey metal desks. The first was occupied by Dr. Bill Newman, who was busily signing a foot-high stack of forms.

Newman looked up. "Thank God, I've been worried 'bout you, thought you'd be here by noon."

"A little trouble on the road, Sir. Jack D'Amico, reporting for duty."

"None of that 'Sir' shit. I'm Bill." He pointed to a chair. "I'll give you a quick rundown on the place."

Bill's words were drawn out in a slow twang, making for a relaxing conversation, whether you wanted to relax or not, definitely not Chicago rat-a-tat-tat. About Jack's height, over six feet, and lanky, handsome in an aw-shucks sort of way. He had grown up on a West Texas ranch outside Marfa. Bussed into town for school in the winter. Cowboyed every summer. University of Texas grad, and proud of it.

Basic rules. Night call rotation—flexible. Mornings—open clinics, first-come, first-seen. Rounds—in-patients before lunch. Usually six to twelve patients, mostly new moms. Afternoons—specialty clinics.

"Broken bones, cast changes, eye injury follow-ups, obstetrics and so on. You've got to be more than a good doctor out here. You have to be part-sociologist, part-historian, even part-genealogist. You better know who's related to whom. Complications like some guys status in the tribe might..." They both heard the sound of screeching brakes at the emergency entrance. "Been expectin' this. Pun intended. Sure glad you're here."

Before they made it to the ER, Bill let him know about a big pow-wow coming up in Gallup. Tomorrow, highlight of the year. Fathers of near-term mothers drove their pregnant wives across rough terrain to induce labor.

"Consider this your initiation to Zuni. Work fast—we only have three delivery rooms."

Albuquerque. Mario talked to anyone who would speak to him at the Public Health office, Bureau of Indian Affairs, the Indian Hospital. What did he learn? Zuni Pueblo was remote compared to other pueblos. And huge—four hundred square miles. Extending into Arizona.

No one heard of Dr. Jack D'Amico. Mario pressed the issue at the PHS and was stone-walled. Talk about body language. He was used to being the intimidator, not on the defensive. But he kept the shit below his shoelaces. Did the job and got out.

Lori May Wilson remained behind as the other mourners, all FBI and/or Chicago police, left the graveside service. Gabriel D'Amico dressed in a dark suit and looking shattered, cried openly, and kept his arms wrapped tightly around himself. He was the only family member present; there were no restaurant staff, no friends, only law enforcement.

Five fresh graves.

Lori took Gabriel's hand. "I'm so very sorry."

Gabriel shook his head and pulled his hand away. His cheeks were wet with tears. An officer waited discretely by an unmarked police car to take him home.

"Can I help you to the car?"

"No, thank you, you are very kind." Gabriel slowly walked away, turning his head back repeatedly as if he couldn't bear to leave.

Lori wondered if the killer or killers were watching. Only two bouquets of flowers, one anonymous (actually the FBI), the other from Gabriel. As instructed, the funeral director placed them in the holes where Rose and Pasquale's caskets lay at rest. She watched workmen fill the graves with soil, but her mind was far from the cemetery.

Thirty-six hours earlier, Lori had been called to the Chicago FBI Field Division in the Loop. The new Dirksen Building on Dearborn Street. Dressed in her FBI uniform—black suit, white blouse buttoned-to-the-top, high heels that she hated. Getting off the elevator at the eighth floor, she wiped her palms on her very short skirt, drew a breath and walked down a long hallway of identical office doors and past the requisite portrait of in-hot-water Richard Milhous Nixon. The desk of a private secretary blocked the entrance of the office of the Special Agent in Charge.

The secretary was on the phone, and after saying repeatedly, "Yes, sir. Yes, sir," she looked up at Lori and smiled. "If you're here to interview as my replacement, you're one floor off. Agent Scott's office is on nine."

"No, actually I'm here to see Special Agent Brooks," said Lori, introducing herself.

"I expected a man, Agent L. M. Wilson. But, you're a pleasant sight. The big boys don't allow many women up here. After thirty years of testosterone and arrogance, I'm glad to be returning to a more hospitable world outside the Service."

Lori guessed the woman to be in her early fifties, maybe older. She couldn't tell by her dark skin and large brown eyes, which were carefully made up. Dark hair cropped short, bound by a black and red scarf. The spot of red being the only real color in the beige office. Her name, according to the plastic plate on her desk, was Yolanda Cervantes, CPA.

"You certainly don't look like you've been here for thirty years," said Lori.

"And you, *mí niña*, look like you're too young, too petite, *y muy chica* to be an agent of the FBI," Yolanda replied, blowing her nose and apologizing. "He keeps it so blasted cold in here, I'm constantly fighting a cold. I don't know why I feel compelled to give you some advice, Agent Wilson. Maybe it's because I'll be out of here soon and he can't do anything else to belittle me. You're about to enter the bullring where that man will find your weak spots, open them like wounds, pour salt on them, eat you up and spit out your tiny bones. He's chewed my skinny butt so many times, I have to sit on a hemorrhoid pillow."

Standing, Yolanda was tall, barely one-hundred-twenty pounds. Quite stately. Long, beautiful legs. By her candor, Lori wondered if she had been drinking, but decided she was high on indignation and using her as a vent, an outlet.

"Forewarned is...."

"*Es cierto*, Agent Wilson. Allow me to escort you. Scream if you need help. I'd love to have the opportunity to catch him brutalizing a female agent and press charges." She took Lori by her arm as if she was going to guide her down the aisle to her own wedding. "I'm a fifth generation American, but he treats me like his maid. *Cuidado, mí niña*, with him. My Grandmother, *gracias a Díos*, used to tell me to squeeze my buttocks tight enough to hold a dime. Then stand up straight and look at my foes in the eyes." Yolanda raised a bronzed hand, tapped at double doors, opened them slightly, and said, "Special Agent Wilson to see you, sir."

"You're on time, Agent Wilson," said Special Agent Brooks, instructing her to take a seat at the table at the end of his corner suite. Next to where the blue and gold flag of the bureau flanked the stars and stripes. Blinds closed, lamps dim. Conservative furniture—leather sofa and matching chairs in front of the desk. A pair of Chinese vases on the conference table. Her first time she had been in the hallowed office. She had no idea why she was there.

"You collect oriental antiques?"

"My wife does. She's Chinese; she has a small shop on Rush Street. Are you interested in oriental stuff?"

"Not at my pay grade."

Brooks held a plastic cup filled with ice. He tossed a few cubes in his mouth. Crunch. Another crunch, like fingernails on a blackboard. His face was as white as his buttondown shirt. Red lips, greying temples.

He swallowed. "You'll be serving the Bureau only on this case. You will answer to me. Everything I say to you is confidential. Do you understand?"

"Yes, sir."

He slid a large manila envelope to her. "Photos of a recent homicide."

She shuffled through the stack of horrific pictures. "What kind of motive or need would the killer possibly have to do this?" Brooks ignored her query. She arranged the photos on the table side-by-side. "Who are they?"

"Wealthy Italians, Pasquale D'Amico, his family, the maid and dog. There is one son not accounted for—he wasn't at home."

One family member at large. A problem for someone. "Who found them?"

"Pasquale's half-brother, Gabriel D'Amico. He says he went by to talk to Pasquale around eight o'clock in the morning. When no one answered the front door, he went around back and found the door unlocked. He called Winnetka police immediately. The chief up there knew the family." Brooks paced the floor, shaking the ice cup, speaking as if she wasn't there. "The chief's a friend of mine from college; he got hold of me right away."

He slid another photo in front of her. "This is Gabriel D'Amico. At this point, he's the only member of the family who knows about the massacre. I told him not to tell anyone anything. There will be no obituaries, nothing."

"He agreed to keep quiet?"

"You bet he did—he knows who I am. He's taking this pretty damn hard. He's rich, I'm told, seems to keep to himself, just a maid and him in a big house. He's not as flamboyant or well known as his brother."

"You said half-brother." Why was the FBI involved? This is a police matter. What did his police friend know? Why the hush-hush? It didn't make sense.

She ran her hand through her long red-brown hair, mahogany in the glow of the indirect lighting. "May I read Gabriel's statement to the police?"

"Basically, it contributes nothing. He described the scene. Gave us a timeline. He was way too upset to make sense."

"I suppose it's too early for the autopsy reports?" asked Lori.

"Right. Now, look, you're going to be square in the middle of this one. This baby is yours—if you're up to it."

"Why me?" She didn't like to be played with. Spit it out, man, what's this all about? Brooks leaned forward, arms crossed. She could smell his cologne. Aramis.

"You're new here, you're not familiar with our ongoing cases, and you don't look like the law. I know you were given the Director's Leadership Award by former-director L. Patrick Gray, not long before he resigned and Director Kelley stepped in." He paused before adding, "You are also very attractive, and your performance package underscores the ability you have to get into places, and close to people...with apparent ease." There was a very pregnant silence between them. "Somehow you gain people's trust."

Brooks was impressed with her looks. Gorgeous. Could be damn good in bed. He lit a cigarette, leaned back in a slouch, his arm over the back of his chair.

"Off the top of your head, any ideas of how to handle this covertly— even if for a few days? The bodies have been removed; the sanitation crew has the scene covered. So, how would you keep a lid on this?"

She turned the pages of the prelim case report. Mrs. D'Amico had been in very poor health. That was it.

"Rose D'Amico became very ill, and on recommendations of her Chicago physician, was flown to a Canadian hospital where a group of specialists were in the midst of a revolutionary way of treating very advanced asthma. The close-knit family went with her."

"Well, I'll be. That's good, girl, very good. I like it." Brooks went back to his desk, pulled a single photo from the desk drawer. "This is the fourth child. Jack D'Amico, or should I say, Doctor Jack D'Amico. All we know is that he's in the military, attached to the Public Health Service. They assigned him to some Indian reservation out west. We got that from Cook County Hospital. They promised us all the Intel on him as soon as they can." He stopped momentarily, drawing on his cigarette, then added, "Can you imagine a major hospital with so little computer automation? They don't even have access codes yet. A patient could be dead for a week before the paper work gets done."

"That could be to our benefit," she commented, her attention focused on the brilliant blue eyes of Jack D'Amico.

11

The long afternoon over, Jack was still marveling at the babies born with a full head of hair. Zuni infants looked more mature than wrinkled WASP babies. He had delivered plenty at Cook County Hospital during his OB tenure. Zuni mothers did all the work. No screaming.

He showered. Jeans, a polo shirt. A quick look at the old rock hospital in the hazy light of dusk. He headed down the dirt street to Newman's house for dinner.

"*Keshshi!*" Bill said. "Welcome, in Zuni-talk." He was wearing a grey T-shirt, bermuda shorts, and tennis shoes. No laces. A can of beer in hand, and a giant, friendly dog at his side. Nothing like the super-efficient physician of an hour earlier. "Coors, or something stronger? I'm partial to Jim Beam myself."

"Beer's fine."

"I don't have much of a repertoire. Hamburgers with *salsa cruda*. A little taste of West-Texas-meets-New-Mexico. First I have to check on Mother."

"Mother?" Jack felt the rhythmic tap of the big dog's tail against his leg.

"This is Flipper, proud Poppa-to be. A Newf, a gentle giant. Newfoundlands—I raise'em. Flapper, the dame, is expecting a litter any time now."

"Seems like everyone's giving birth around here."

After making sure the soon-to-deliver Flapper was okay, Bill deftly diced an onion, a tomato, a small jalapeño. A dash of vinegar, water, salt, fresh cilantro. Loading a scoop of the salsa on a tostada, he offered it to Jack. "If you've never had this before, brother, prepare to become addicted."

"I had some Hatch green chile in Grants," Jack said between crunches. "Whew—this is dyn-o-mite."

"You ain't just a woofin'." Bill turned to molding the ground beef into patties. "On the ranch where I grew up they had a cook, Barbara was her name, that took care of all us cowboys during the gatherings. Man, could she ride. She told me the secret to a great hamburger is not to smash the meat together. And don't poke at it ever. On her day off, she rode topless—no kidding."

"Get real."

"Honest. She was wicked."

The cast-iron skillet was hot. He shoveled the meat, two inches-thick, one-half pound each, into the pan. "Medium rare?" Jack nodded, scooped up more salsa, chasing it with beer. "I've learned to ignore the cooking process, keep busy doing something else." He sliced an avocado in half, popped the seed out with a knife, scored the lime green flesh, and scooped the avocado out, dividing it between two buns. In a flash, the meat was turned, on the buns and smothered with salsa. They sat at the kitchen table, white Formica with stainless steel trim. Like everything in the tract house, an heirloom of the fifties.

"Awesome. Best hamburger I've ever had," said Jack with his mouth full.

"You're just hungry."

"No, I mean it. My Dad has a restaurant."

Bill fished two beers out of the frig. "Let's move to the living room, put on some records."

A LP dropped from the stack on to the turntable. Bill held up the album cover.

"Perfect, I'm into all the folk stuff, back to Guthrie, Seeger."

Bill kicked off his tennis shoes, dropped to the floor, propped up against the wall. Jack took the only chair. A rickety folding chair with sagging plastic strips.

Bill talked about himself. He wanted to be a country GP. That was the rub. His girlfriend wanted him to be a surgeon.

"I met her freshman year. She was a cheerleader at UT. Wore white boots—the whole Jane Fonda look. Well, before Jane went to North Vietnam last summer. At first she wanted to live in a city like Dallas or Houston, have a big social life, join the Junior League, travel the world. I just wanted to jump her bones. Then came '67. The Summer of Love in the Haight. She talked me into taking a Greyhound bus up there.

"I'll go with love and liberation, but you can't build a society on drugs. My babe was—she thought—a purist. I realized she was just snooty. Her left-wing politics and esoteric aesthetics. All a farce. Seemed to me that everyone was interested in two things—overthrow the government and screwing."

Jack laughed. "Relevant. And tempting."

"Tell me about it. She fell for it, all of it. She left me. You know, she was so beautiful—could have modeled for I. Magnin. I ended up volunteering at a free clinic. Treated kids suffering from bad acid trips or VD."

"The Haight was an egalitarian bubble," said Jack.

"That's heavy. So cynical already?"

"I went to a Jesuit school. My best friend was in Vietnam—101st Airborne paratrooper. We tripped together, got into The Grateful Dead, Jerry Garcia. But in the end, I wasn't impressed. Like you just said, it was all about drugs and sex. Hey man, what's worse? Rebelling against the robots of the fifties or the cheating businessman knocking back martinis in the sixties?"

"Don't ask me. I'm Episcopalian."

"Turn up the music," Jack said.

"You got it. And it's time for some bourbon." Bill took a bottle and glasses from a kitchen cabinet and poured a generous measure, then set the bottle between them on the floor.

Bill settled in. Record albums and protective sheets covered the carpet.

"Back to the Zunis. Like I said earlier, I really like them. Here I am, this youngblood from Texas. So I come up with this idea to serve up a real barbeque for all the staff. Brisket, beans, coleslaw, hot dogs for the kids. Mustard, catsup, the whole nine yards. Damn if the Indians didn't sit around the perimeter of my dinky backyard. Some on chairs that they brought themselves. Some sat cross-legged on the grass. Quiet. Polite. Sort of Zen. Not like any of my wild buddies back home.

"One time we loaded beer—I mean cases of beer—into a stock tank. Iced it down. This one dude comes walking by and says, 'Y'all watch over me—I may end up in that tank tonight.'"

Jack laughed. Reached for the bourbon bottle. Bill kept on rolling.

"What I'm saying is I'm copasetic with the Zuni people. It's not that they didn't have fun for sure. They just seemed more respectful—at peace. When they left, the place was pristine."

Bill emptied his glass, saying, "Hey, Jack, you're gonna like it here."

"Midnight," said Jack finally, rising to his feet. "We gotta work tomorrow."

"Five AM."

"Rounds?"

"No. I'm going to take you up for a ride. Give you a feel for the country. Good little two-seater Piper Cub over at the FAA. Can you dig it?"

Jack left, feeling a light buzz. More bothersome, he had a stiff neck. An aching in his bones. Too young for this, he thought. Was he reacting to the altitude? Six-hundred feet above sea level in Chicago, versus six-thousand in Zuni. Pretty damn big difference. He shivered. Ground fog was creeping in, drifting off the lake.

Lori worked better on a full stomach. She walked the three-and-a-half blocks down State Street to Marshall Field. Over a bowl of chowder in the restaurant, she thought about the tragic photos. She was still bothered about the secrecy. She didn't mind going in alone, in fact, she preferred it. No cheerleader or sorority life for her. No rah-rah. Really not many friends. But she wasn't being told everything—she could be sent in as a sacrificial lamb. Still, she had been handed a major case.

She reached for the check—a hand clasped her shoulder.

"Easy, there, Agent Wilson, it's just me. We meet again," said Yolanda Cervantes. "I'm on lunch break. ¿Que pasa con Agent Brooks?"

"Have a seat. I survived." She told Yolanda, who asked to be called 'Yolie,' that Brooks was blunt, old school. "He put me in my place. Then he gave me a case. He's letting me run with it."

"Unreal. I'm blown away. That pig gave you a case—no offense, but he's..."

"No offense taken. I wondered that myself."

Yolanda folded her manicured hands on her lap. "If I were you, I'd think long and hard about each and every word that man says to you."

Class B khaki uniform on, and hungry. Bill's hamburger from the night before was long gone. He was still creaky. Must be a storm on the way.

Jack opened every cabinet, hoping the last occupant had left something. Literally, the cupboards were bare. He fished some 'borrowed' tea bags from the Albuquerque motel from his dopp kit. The PHS had graciously supplied a skeleton collection of pots (1), pans (1), and some utensils. One big spoon. One small spoon. Chipped Fiesta ware. Two dented tin cups.

Carrying his tea (no sugar), he checked out his new quarters. Small living room. Fireplace, a plus. He poured a second cup of weak tea, went

 47

into what he supposed was a mud room. One door led to a detached garage, another to the basement. Flipped on the outdoor switch and stepped into the pale pre-dawn darkness. Breathed in the scent of scrub pine and juniper. Brushing by a clump of purple thistles, he noticed beaded moisture on the flower heads glinting in the light of the back door. He lifted the door of the single car garage, pulled the string attached to a bare bulb. Grimy cabinets filled with paint, snow chains, empty oil cans, empty jugs of antifreeze. The cabinet door suddenly came loose from the hinges and crashed to the floor. He jumped back, spilling tea on his trousers. Ducking back outside, he saw headlights. Bill in a dusty VW van.

"Up for some flyin'?"

"Right on."

Bill drove out of the compound to a lone building which housed the FAA presence in the region. En route he explained that the facility was small, but it did a lot—directing all aircraft between Phoenix and Albuquerque.

"Easy to get lost. Lots of real estate. Few landmarks. One mountain after another—they all look alike. Not to the Zunis, of course. They have an amazing capacity to comprehend space. Did you know the Zuni World has six directions? North, South, East, West, Above and Below."

"I'm lost with just four," laughed Jack.

After a ' howdy, good mornin' tuya' to the air controller, they walked to the red Piper. Bill primed the engine, hand-turned the propeller. Got it going on the second try, sending vibrations through the cockpit.

It was a cool morning—lots of moisture, patchy clouds. Take-off was bumpy. Noisy. Leveling at two-thousand feet, Bill pointed out Sacred Mountain and two other towering projections hovering in an indigo-infused light. "There's a trailhead up there in the Zuni mountains, loops on three successive mesas. A spectacular overlook. Too cloudy to see it today. There was a strong thermal inversion during the night. Centered right over the Zuni Forest. We could have a real light show this morning."

"Wish I had a camera," said Jack.

"You'd need an extra-wide lens."

Jack settled in, ready to grasp the vast, seemingly endless panorama spread beneath them. Primitive single-tracks, logging railroad corridors, two-track forest roads. He spotted a dust trail. Sheep herds. Wild horses. Miles and miles of grassland. Deep cobalt-purple shadows engulfed the depths of red earth canyons. To their east, the rising sun eased over the horizon. A shadow cast by Lookout Mountain onto a low cloudbank looked huge. An immense angular specter from his perspective.

The gently sloping forest began to climb in altitude. They were flying through ever-changing layers of air with varying densities. Light rays bent on the curve toward high-density cool air. Warmer, less dense air on the outside began to refract. Literally, out of thin air, the energized rays caused everything to change. At wildly different angles, the metamorphosed light re-cast "normal" accepted visible reality into an otherworldly spectacle.

In seconds. A flash. Flutter. Out of focus. Rational surroundings became shifty, elusive. Physical landmarks began to vanish. Appear where they were not. A wind-carved vertical tower of red and cream sandstone elongated. Striations multiplied like red and white- striped lighthouses guarding the coasts. Another compressed. Inverted. Shortened. Multiplied.

Forests loomed, then receded. Towering cliffs sank into water. There was no water.

Jack felt isolated, yet engulfed. As the plane changed altitude, the visual effect was magnified over the huge distances, exaggerating the vertical distortion, displacing images. Light was not reflecting. It was refracting. Bending.

A far-off mesa topped by dark lava vanished as light deflected over Jack's head. Was it all a mirage or an illusion? Fantastic sequences flashed in Technicolor like a fast-paced dream. He sensed a sound. A sound like a heartbeat. In seconds, he saw duplications. Distortions. He felt like he was in a wavy-mirrored funhouse. Which image was real? Every ground object he could see was shifting. Was there just one mesa? Or six or seven?

"I will remember this," said Jack. "Awesome."

"Optical physics, amigo," said Bill. "The team of light and air." He put the plane in a wide arc to turn back, saying over the din of the engine, "Another day I'll take you over to El Morro, Inscription Rock, but we better get to work."

Rounds began right on time. They were joined by a third physician, back from a two-week leave. A pleasant-enough guy, red-haired, very little to say, but showing a clear disdain for his Indian patients. Seems the guy spent his free time in his trailer with his wife and new baby. This was going to be a Bill-and-Jack operation.

Bill called for a lunch break and headed home to check on Flapper. Jack closed the door to the office and called Winnetka. Twenty-two rings and no answer. He dialed the lake house. No answer. They could be out on the lake, but Jo Lou didn't like the water at all, so why wasn't she answering?

A metal door down the hall slammed way too loudly. Shaking a sudden chill down his neck, he felt like his family was very far away. He closed the venetian blinds, a dusty shadow angled across a pile of charts. He put his hands in his lab coat, noticing for the first time a row of eight-by-ten black and white photographs simply framed in thin black wood with extra-wide mats. Western ranch scenes. A worn boot in a stirrup. Two unsmiling boys with snap button shirts and big-brimmed hats. Silhouetted horses galloping across a dark ridge, lightning in the background.

So Dr. Bill was artistic besides being a pilot. Way cool.

Admiral Zeller put down a notepad filled with his own kind of short-hand and lit a Lucky Strike. He had spent much of the morning on the phone, first with the Chicago police, then a call from the FBI. Not much information from either of them, nothing to point to a motive for killing an entire family—almost an entire family. Zeller knew full well there was much more to this case. The hush-hush, the FBI, for godsake. Neither agency provided a reason for wanting him to protect Jack. What did Jack know that would place him in harm's way? That someone wants him dead. And how in the hell was he going to protect him?

The head of Cook County Hospital records was a self-important, grossly overweight woman, tough-as-nails, ready to give out nothing. Lori acted as if she was being drawn into a conspiracy, one which could bring down a doctor.

The woman responded in a whisper. She opened Jack D'Amico's file, pointing to the form indicating his last salary check had gone to an address in Albuquerque, New Mexico—Forward as Necessary.

Not much, but something. The woman added that a man had called earlier in the week asking for the same guy. A secretary who fielded the call had just returned from maternity leave and should have known better, but she had told the man the doctor was on his way to another assignment in New Mexico. The man wanted his forwarding address. At first, the secretary balked, then agreed to check his file.

"Did she give it to him?" The woman shrugged.

From a pay phone, Lori told Brooks what she had learned. "Is there anything new that I need to know?"

"Nope," said Brooks.

"I'm going to New Mexico, Albuquerque first, then Indian country."

"You still think you can handle this case?"

"Yes, sir."

"Can you shoot?"

Lori cleared her throat. "I am an expert. What about back-up?"

"You're it. Brass in DC said to keep it low profile."

Brooks pressed his intercom. "Miss Cervantes, take care of whatever Agent Wilson needs."

"Certainly, whatever she needs."

The Chicago Division Office alerted Zeller that Jack's car had been stolen. The APB had been picked up by the Kansas FBI Division. Someone sharp also noticed two speeding tickets for an Illinois-registered driver, not Jack, on US 54. Further, Cook County Hospital acknowledged Jack's destination was Zeller's office. US 54—a direct run to New Mexico.

Zeller walked down the hall and poked his head in Dr. Martin's office. "What was that you told me earlier, our doctor at the Jicarilla Apache Med center?"

"Doctor Davis had to be rushed to Albuquerque. Acute appendicitis," Martin answered.

"Perfect. Up near the Colorado border. I've got you a replacement," Zeller said, already walking back to his office.

He got the head doctor at Zuni, saying, "Bill, send D'Amico to Dulce, ASAP. Have him use one of the Gallup motor pool cars. Tell him to lock that Jeep of his in a garage—you're worried about car theft."

Yolanda booked Lori on United through Denver, telling her she was from Aurora, south of the city. "Not the Hispanic ghetto. My father runs a grocery store; brought in produce other suppliers couldn't get from Mexico. Poblanos, jalapeños, mangos, papayas, avocados, jicima. You name it. He predicts a Mexican-food craze is on the horizon."

"Are you going back there after you retire?" asked Lori.

"Sí, como no. Of course. After September first, I'm heading home, start my own accounting practice—Cervantes, Esq. LLC, CPA.

They both heard Brooks' door slam—they tightened as he walked by. Without looking at either, he slid a file toward Yolanda. "I think both of you pretty things have more to do than chat. Schedule me for a massage and manicure. Then I'll be at the club, dinner with Senator Trask. No calls unless it's urgent. Do call my wife, the usual excuse."

When the elevator doors closed, Yolanda practically spit the words, "Enjoy your martinis, asshole." She darted her brown eyes at Lori and snapped, "That man uses me like toilet paper."

Lori laughed. "Don't let it get to you. Just keep on pickin' cotton."

"Whatever. I do find it exhilarating that *el cabrón* trusts me. I may be treated like chewing gum on his shoe, but I see, and I remember everything he does.

"Okay now, your flight leaves O'Hare at eleven-forty-five in the morning. In Albuquerque, you will be met by a friend of mine, from my old college days. He's way cool. He's also the one who steered me into the FBI. I'll be tracking you, keep in touch."

At the Albuquerque Sun Port she was met by a fifty-ish agent with buzz-cut greying hair and a limp. Worn Levi's, a tan shirt, dark glasses. A badge on his chest, gun in a black holster at his belt. His tan face was as worn as the jeans.

He introduced himself as Josh Flores, a forest ranger based in the Mt. Taylor District of the Cibola National Forest. A huge territory, 1.6 million acres.

As they walked out of the airport, he said, "Yolie told me to look out for you, but I don't know what you're working on, and I don't want to know. When I leave you, you're on your own." He led her to a battered green truck with a Department of Agriculture/Forestry Service shield on the door. "I've done some prelim work for you. Hop in."

"Where are we headed?" asked Lori.

"My pad. Grants."

"I expected an undercover agent."

Josh smiled wryly. "Maybe I am."

Route 66 was nearly empty. An occasional big rig heading for the coast. He pushed the pickup, making risky passes on double yellow lines. A small leather pouch, tightly cinched, swayed back and forth on the rear view mirror.

Josh caught her glance and said, "I'm in good with the Bureau of

Indian Affairs. Made nice with the chief. He gave me that to protect me. Hey, it can't hurt. I'll try anything."

"Yolie said you two met in college."

"I'm older—met her when she was a freshman and I was about to graduate."

"You dated her?"

"Totally. We did some real fine boot-scootin' together. Course that was before I got reamed."

"So after UNM, you went into the FBI?"

"Later. Like you, I got a master's in criminal justice. Georgetown."

"And that prepared you to be in the Forestry Service?"

"I'll tell you about that later. We're home," said Josh. He pulled in under an awning next to a drive-in window, a FDIC sticker still on the glass. A grey International Scout was parked in the next bay in front of an old Jeep Wagoneer.

"You live in a branch bank?"

"Well, it's better than a Dairy Queen. The bank got a contract with the Laguna tribe and needed a bigger building. I got it cheap. Actually it has everything I need."

He opened a thick double-paned glass door into a vestibule filled with rangy red geraniums. Another security door led to the waiting area. A couch, a table. A cheap stained wall heater. Cardboard boxes everywhere, brimming with files. Recessed ceiling fixtures glowed down on the teller counter, a/k/a the kitchen. The truck and SUVs were in view through the teller windows.

"My bedroom was the manager's office." He limped across the room and pointed down a hallway. "Down there I have my very own vault." He reached behind the bedroom door and handed her a bullet-proof vest. "FBI-issue. Whoa—it's way too big for you, but it will still stop a bullet."

Lori laughed. "I feel like a rodeo clown inside a padded rain barrel."

"When I quote-unquote 'left' the FBI, I gave them some bologna about all my equipment getting fried. Then I kept it." He handed her a set of keys. "The Scout is yours.

Everything you need is in there. A quick look, and I've got to go."

Raid jacket. Enough evidence equipment to process a large crime scene. Assault rifle in a roof-rack. "That police radio will connect you to tribal police or dispatcher. I'm always out in nowhere, but they usually can find me."

She followed him to a junction. He thrust his arm out his window, gesturing straight ahead—Route 66 to Gallup. He turned south onto State Route 547. It was dark when she pulled into Gallup. Thank goodness Flores had made a reservation.

El Rancho Hotel. Like a faded postcard. Past its time, but a place to park. An elderly Indian was polishing the shoes of a heavyset man sitting in one of the leather high chairs. Ponderous log furniture. A huge *Yei-bi-chai* Navajo rug. Mounted deer and antelope heads. Unique background music, low sounds of Indians chanting, drumming.

She was more interested in eating. The desk clerk told her the restaurant had closed for the night, but the 49er Bar was still serving.

She could use a drink.

Seated in a red leather booth, she ordered a bourbon and water.

"Short or tall?" asked the waitress.

Lori laughed, saying, "Better make it tall. I've wanted to be tall all my life."

"And to eat?"

"The biggest steak you've got, rare."

"You got it, girl."

The television behind the bar, despite the snowy picture, occupied the attention of a cowboy with long sideburns, moustache, and Stetson. A spokesman was saying the White House had sent a letter to the Oglala Sioux chiefs promising to discuss the Fort Laramie Treaty.

A pair of inebriated Indians at the bar began shouting and slamming down their bottles of Budweiser. "We stand by our brothers and sisters at Wounded Knee." Then more insults. "We curse the FBI. Stinking pigs!"

She turned away. The American Indian Movement versus the FBI, BIA, Federal Marshalls, local Police. Gun battles, tear gas barrages, fire-fights. Almost a full-scale military offensive. A dark period in the Dakotas.

At least the drink was strong. She learned to drink at the University of Colorado. Her father, a Methodist minister, would have whooped her if he had known. Home was southeastern Colorado. La Junta. Flat plains, wind-driven snow. Space. He taught her to hunt and fish. His parish pay was paltry—he justified the hunting because the family needed food.

He taught her how to gut an elk, skin a rabbit, filet trout. Make elk sausage, rabbit stew. But she was no hick. A scholarship got her a master's at Harvard. That was where she shared a tiny apartment and a bedroll with her dog, Bo. She existed on cottage cheese and ketchup. Saltine crackers and mustard.

Thankfully, the steak arrived.

12

Jack read the temporary reassignment orders. "What the shit? I just got here."

Bill gave him a letter of introduction, and orders for a car, adding, "I've got you a ride into Gallup—the pharmacist is heading into town to pick up stuff."

Stan drove a faded red VW bug with ratty seats. He turned out to be a talker, a big guy with thinning grey hair and bushy sideburns. His pharmacy jacket barely buttoned over his gut.

At Vanderwagen, he pulled in to pick up his mail. The post office was inside the White Water Trading Post, on the left.

Jack wandered past the silversmithing area. Findings, silver. Drills, polishing machines. Turquoise, coral, bone, agate, shells, and amethyst. All in bins, sold by the pound. Zunis, as well as two Navajo women in long skirts, waited at the pawn counter.

The trading post had it all: blankets, saddles, rifles, chainsaws. Jack needed only one thing—sustenance. He spotted a couple of shelves of foodstuffs in a small room. Skirting the pawn line, he almost tripped over a drunk propped up in the corner.

"Sorry, I didn't see you."

The man, who was probably thirty but looked sixty, slurred, "Why did you do this to me?"

"What?" Jack leaned closer. The man's hands were shaking and tears were running down his cheeks.

"I'm gonna go crazy. Buy me a beer..."

"What you need is a shower and some food. Get a job."

"If I had a job, man, I'd get my wife back. Get my family..."

A woman, her face creased and leathered, said, "Come on, Earl, coffee in the truck."

He helped lug the guy to his feet. The man kept muttering 'Lost my place in line.' Jack snapped up a loaf of fry bread, paid for it, and was in the VW before Stan showed up.

"I saw you met Earl," said Stan, turning on to the highway. "Since his brother was killed in Vietnam, he's never spent more than a week outside of jail. It's the whiskey. Some winter he's going to freeze to death."

Jack and his twenty-five cent fry bread left Gallup just before two o'clock in a USPHS-labeled white Chevrolet, ready to take over as the only doctor available for the whole damn Jicarilla Apache nation.

Mario checked out a dozen trading posts in Gallup. He had to step over a half-dozen drunks in the space of an hour, and was disgusted and angry by the time he finally hit on something at a spot in the road called Vanderwagen. A hung-over Zuni remembered being in line, trying to pawn a necklace. Mario dropped a five in his lap. It disappeared. An Anglo, "Blue Eyes," the man called him, bought fry bread. Mario pressed for more—what was he driving, which way did he head. All he got was a blank look. Indians were good at that.

A platinum-blonde woman with a beehive hairdo came out of the walk-in vault. Seeing Mario, she asked if he needed help.

"No, I got what I needed. Tell me, do the Indians around here get drunk every weekend?"

"Around here every day is a weekend," she responded.

Mario slammed the screen door of the trading post behind him, stubbing his toe on the iron bars. The wheels of his car spewed gravel as he headed toward Zuni.

Jack drove north on Route 666 to Shiprock, toward Farmington. He was in Navajo country. A hexagonal hogan beside every house. His mind drifted. The lake house. Silver Bay. Lake Superior, more like the Atlantic Ocean than a lake. The opposite of the parched expanse in front of him. Desolate, windblown.

The road was bad; he was detoured repeatedly to the side of the pockmarked pavement. He passed a solitary Indian. Where was he headed? There wasn't a dwelling in sight. What do they do out here? Herd sheep, craft jewelry. Make babies for the white doctors to deliver.

Crownpoint and Kayente to the west. Monument Valley in the distance. No trees, no gardens. An occasional trailer, truck. Ramshackle fencing, a hogan. The light crystalized, a mirage appeared out of nowhere. He was in it. The light was mind-boggling, reaching his eyes with a fluttering effect. A shimmer. Scintillation and shimmer. He had never experienced such a clear head.

East at Shiprock, rumbling onto a steel-structured bridge over the San Juan River. Irrigated fields of alfalfa and corn. He left the Navajo Reservation and began climbing in altitude. Zigzag turns, steep drop-offs. A twisted guardrail left a precipitous gap. An unnecessary sign warned of 'Dangerous Driving Conditions During Inclement Weather.' More signs warned of 6% (sharp) downgrades, (sharp) curves, rock slides.

The land broadened into vast meadows. He was on the Jicarilla Apache reservation. The clinic, surrounded by pine trees, was easy to spot. A woman wearing a plaid shirt with snap buttons and faded Levis was sitting on the steps. Black hair bound in a knot. Coral earrings matched the blouse. As he approached, she pulled on a white lab coat.

"Hi Doc. I'm Gloria. Lots of sick kids," she said with no inflection, and led him to three young patients, aged six to ten.

High fever, red throats, whitish-yellow exudates on the tonsils and back of the throat. Difficulty swallowing, swollen lymph glands in the neck. He told Gloria to swab for cultures. The kids were quiet, even when he coated their throats with gentian violet.

It was late when they locked up. Gloria gave him the key for the doctor's residence across the street. He tossed the few belongings he had in an unused bedroom, then discovered a T-bone steak and some tater tots in the freezer. Things were looking up. He heard a knock on the door.

He was met with the stare of a large man, hair braided, a red band tied around his head. "You new doctor?"

"Yes, Doctor D'Amico. I'll..."

"I'm chief of Jicarilla tribe. Cousin to Toklanni, big shot at Mescalero Apache Reservation."

In a voice devoid of expression, the man proceeded to tell Jack what would be expected of him. The gist of which was not to interfere with the traditions of the Jicarillas. The chief simply turned and left on foot.

Door closed, Jack said out loud, "Hum. What was that all about?"

He fired up a grill on the concrete patio in the back, 'borrowed' a can of Coors, turned on the radio. He twisted the dial. Only Radio Free Europe.

A twenty-minute wait for the charcoal to burn down. He called the lake house. No answer. Next, Winnetka. No luck. He could call the restaurant, but hesitated. Too late, plus he didn't really know any of his father's employees. Pasquale kept the business side of his life separate from his family. He and Nic should have worked as dishwashers or bus boys, or waited tables. No. Pasquale had other ideas, and not soft ones.

He sent them Outward Bound, to learn survival skills. The only thing they knew about the restaurant business was to tip at least twenty percent.

The steak was over the coals. He ripped off a chunk of fry bread, opened another beer and tried out a rickety director's chair. The canvas sagged, but held. The bread was sour, but not bad.

Two 'stars' near the horizon, rather than the zenith, glowed steadily. Planets, he knew, they don't flicker. The clarity of the night sky was as exquisite as being in the mirage. A sense of peace swept over him. For the second time today.

Lori awakened to the sound of a vacuum cleaner in the hall, a long hall, a vacuum cleaner not exactly working right. She never slept so hard—was it the bourbon or the Navajo tea?

A fitted white shirt, tied above low-waisted jeans. Sandals. No time for breakfast. The Zuni hospital was her first stop.

Dr. Bill Newman was immediately taken. She was flat-out beautiful. He found it hard to pay attention to what she was saying. "What was that you said?"

"Jack and I are going to get married," Lori repeated.

"What?" Bill said abruptly. "He didn't tell me."

"As soon as he finishes his tour of duty and is accepted into a residency." He was mentally undressing her. "I'm here to surprise him. I just can't be away from him for any length of time—do you understand?"

Bill certainly understood, and told her she was a bit late. Head of Area Office had sent Jack on a temp assignment.

Lori stepped close to Bill, who was now transfixed by her appearance. "Well?"

"Well what?"

"Come on, where is Jack?"

"Lady, this is the military. Do you understand?" He paused, watching her fixed expression. "Need-to-know basis."

Lori leaned forward, placed both hands on his desk. Knew his eyes were on her cleavage. She didn't dare tell him she was FBI. Not yet. She stepped back, looking at his face, not eyes, and said, "I'm pregnant."

"Pregnant?"

"Yes. He doesn't know."

Suddenly, they both felt a tremor. A pencil rolled across Bill's desk. He caught it.

"What was that?" asked Lori.

"Lots of seismic activity around here." And slipping plates, he thought, especially along the Continental Divide. He tapped the pencil on the desk, picturing flight maps in his head. A fault—north/south fracture just east of Dulce. Christ, Jack needs to know. He felt her gaze shift from his face to his eyes. And from his eyes to a place inside him that she understood. "Okay. He's in Apache country, PHS clinic in Dulce. Up north, right on..."

"The Colorado border," said Lori.

She left the hospital thankful Dr. Bill was a sensitive guy. On a hunch, she drove toward the pueblo.

Jack was met with a traffic jam. Trucks, mainly Ford pick-ups, parked all around the clinic. "What the hell?" Patients were standing in line, trailing out the door. "What's going on?"

"High fevers, red throats. Like yesterday, white-ish yellow puss on the back of the throat," answered Gloria.

"Sounds like strep throat," he said, shrugging on a lab coat. His first patient was a five-year-old boy. "I'm going to swab some of the exudate on the tonsillar pillars. Make a smear with one, and plate the other on blood agar." Gloria nodded.

He took one look at the slide. Myriads of strands and couplets of spherical organisms—all stained gram positive. "His temp?"

"One-hundred-and-three."

"It'll take twenty-four hours for the agar culture, but this is strep, no doubt. I'll use penicillin, unless the antibiotic sensitivities say otherwise when we get them in a couple of days."

It didn't take long for him to find out what the clinic had in stock. Five vials of procaine penicillin. Enough to treat a third of the patients already at the clinic. God knows how many more to come.

He called the PHS hospital in Albuquerque. The consequences of inadequate or non-treatment of Type-2 strep could be disastrous. The next epidemic would be rheumatic fever. Associated heart problems. Renal disease. He could expect deaths in the very young and very old. Albuquerque promised to fly in supplies by the next morning.

By the end of the day, he had seen more than a hundred patients.

He had antibiotics for twenty-five or thirty. They sterilized the clinic as best they could. He didn't think some would return.

Dinner. Exhaustion. He plied open a can of tomato soup with a bottle opener, heated it in a cast-iron skillet, and retreated to the porch. A black night.

Suddenly the night sound of living things stopped—no crickets, no barking dogs. Only silence.

He stood dead still. When he stepped inside the house, the power went off. A monstrous cracking sound ricocheted. He was lifted off his feet and sent crashing to the floor. The walls of the living room separated at one corner. Walls shuddered, the floor reverberated. With a deafening bang, the walls slammed together again.

He crawled for the dining table and spread himself flat. Shaking continued for more than a minute. Then came stability, and with it, silence.

"Earthquake," Jack said aloud. "What a godforsaken dump. Filled with goddamn superstitious, stone-faced, burro-headed Indians. And now this."

A knock at the door stopped his tirade. The door was jammed and he had to give it several kicks and a violent jerk to get it open. Gloria was standing there, composed as though nothing had happened.

All she said was, "Happened before, mountain gods very unhappy." She handed him a battery-powered lantern.

Jack brushed past her. The clinic door was broken off the hinges. In the darkness, he worked his way to the pharmacy. He slipped, reached out to regain his balance, and sent a stainless steel tray flying. The white metal cabinets had crashed to the floor. Pills and broken glass covered the linoleum tiles. The X-ray machine had been tossed across the room and bent in the middle by the 7-point-magnitude quake.

Without thinking, he picked up a phone. No dial tone.

Admiral Zeller was awakened by a phone call from the state police. Dulce had sustained a Richter 6.9 earthquake, larger than the one five years earlier.

"Any information on the clinic? Any fatalities?"

"Nothing confirmed. It's too remote."

After hanging up, he sat on the side of the bed, groping for a pack of cigarettes. His wife asked him what was wrong.

"That poor guy," was all Zeller could say.

Farmington, nearly ninety miles away, had experienced the tremor. Mario bolted from bed, cursing New Mexico. His inclination was to get in the car and get the hell out of the damned state and back to civilization.

Down the street in another motel, Lori sat up in bed, feeling the rumbles. Distant, and fading. She would ask about it in the morning.

Tito roused, his body absorbing the earth's rumbling, though it was occurring some one-hundred-and-thirty miles away. Opening his eyes, he saw his father standing at his bedside, silhouetted against the light in the hospital hall.

Louis Paul held the flat palm of one hand over him. "Still, my son, the gods are anxious about something. Listen."

13

Mario shaved, occasionally glancing at the small bathroom window, hoping to see some daylight. He told the desk clerk he would be staying another night.

At a truck stop on the outskirts of town, he ate a breakfast burrito. He spoke to no one. Driving east on US 64, he cursed as the sun rose—he was driving straight into it. Barely seven in the morning.

Lori's alarm went off at seven o'clock. Her stomach growled. She dressed quickly and headed down the street. *Huevos rancheros* at Lupe's Restaurant. Everyone, especially Lupe, was talking about the earthquake. She also overhead a delivery man say he had talked to his sister in Dulce the day before, and everyone on the reservation was coming down with some awful bug. People were really sick, and that was before the earthquake.

She finally picked up a local radio station in the SUV. A dead-pan voice said, "The epicenter was the Jicarilla Apace village of Dulce, eleven miles from the Colorado border, in a remote mountainous region. The U.S. Geological Survey said the initial quake measured 7.5 magnitude at about 11:30 PM. and a 5.2 magnitude aftershock two hours later.

"Ambulances from as far away as Farmington to the west and Taos to the east are currently attempting to reach the vicinity."

Off came the sandals, on went hiking boots. Shopping for supplies, water, groceries. A Styrofoam cooler and ice. When she got on the highway, the sun was high in the sky.

State police cars re-routed all traffic at mile marker 127, detouring around a buckled gap in the pavement. Mario's car dragged bottom, letting out a steel-screeching scream. He had to whip the wheel to avoid boulders. The car groaned down the main and only paved street in town. Power company workmen leaned against their trucks, sharing coffee from thermoses with telephone linemen. The air smelled of diesel fuel. Belching D-Cats attempted to clear a side road.

It was easy to find the PHS clinic—pickups packed the lot. He counted three exits, then parked behind a dense stand of junipers. He tore off strips of red duct tape with his teeth, creating a cross on his aluminum-sided gun case. Makeshift, but real enough to get around the line and into the packed waiting room.

At the reception window, he said, "I'm from Albuquerque, and..."

The nurse interrupted him, saying, "You have our medicine?"

"No. I'm here to evaluate the situation. Your doctor...the new one, I need to talk to him personally."

"Doctor busy. We got the clinic straightened up, but no power or water. But we're lucky. Police won't let some people back into their own houses."

"The damage is that bad?"

"Eleven people died...so far. Quake left crack in the dam up on mountain—water and rocks came down, tore up sewer lines, everything in the way."

"When do you think I could catch the doctor?"

"House calls all afternoon. Sick kids can't get here. He's staying across the street. He'll be late. Do you have a card, an ID?"

He was gone. She shrugged and turned back to the quiet but anxious eyes of the patients, all staring directly at her.

Just before noon, Lori told the same nurse she was a field medic from Taos. She got the same story.

"I'll try to connect with him later," Lori said.

"You'll have to get in line. Another man was here couple hours ago. From Area Office."

"Did you get his name? Maybe I know him."

"No." She looked past her. "We are busy."

Back in the Scout, she wondered how Zeller could have gotten a man up there so quickly. Had someone driven all night? No way. She picked up the radio transmitter.

Slumped behind the wheel, Mario watched the clinic, eyes only looking for a doctor-type. That was until a hot-looking woman came and went. Anglo. Probably another care-giver for the Indians, paid for with tax-payer money.

14

The Jahata home was centered in a five-and-six-tiered earthen quadrangle, a complicated maze of twelve-hundred rooms, housing over one-hundred families. In the early 1800s the narrow streets were like dark tunnels. Multistory levels were stacked over the alley-like maze of passageways.

Tito was back in the pueblo only days after the accident. No use arguing with a *shiwani*. Not one as powerful as Louis Paul Jahata.

Louis Paul removed the cast from his arm immediately. Skin marbled red and purple. Hot to the touch. Clear evidence of infection. He had anticipated such, and already had prepared a poultice. Prickly pear (to lessen pain and inflammation). Red root (to aid in circulation by generating capillaries). Hollyhock (to increase the ferocity of his white blood cells' ability to grab bacteria). Spikenard (an antibacterial agent).

He blessed a long, five-inch-wide bear-hide thong, and wrapped it around Tito's ripped arm and blackened hand.

Vervain mint tea. Sleep.

Louis Paul began a narrative, a re-education to ground his son's recovery in the Zuni of the past. It made little difference. Tito was in a twilight zone. The tea. "A very long time ago, our people made homes, only to move after violent shaking of Mother Earth."

In a mesmerizing cadence, he told of previous Zuni settlements. Northern California. Utah. Arizona. Northern New Mexico. Each historic move prompted by earthquakes, interpreted as the anger of the gods.

"Today, we inhabit *Hawikku*, reverently known as *Halona Idiwan'a*, the Middle Place of the World." As he talked, Tito's eyelids fluttered, unintelligible sounds came from his mouth through clinched teeth. Touching his forehead, he murmured, "Rest, my son."

He turned to look down past ladders and chimney pipes down to a large packed-dirt plaza below, the heart of the pueblo. He was worried, not about Tito. He had felt a tremor in the night.

Natural forces. Very mysterious. Powerful. The most ancient deities reside in the Earth Below. Though unseen, a deity was sending a message.

He sat cross-legged, allowing himself to slip into a light trance. Open to Zuni cosmology, he connected to a power infinitely greater than his own limited human strength. He entered a formless mist. Solar alignments became fluid and crystallized. The moon cycle shifted in the traffic. There was chaos in the Earth Below. A warning. The vision came into focus for a millisecond. He saw a white man's face, blue eyes. Something was wrong. Very wrong.

The uphill road to the hospital in Black Rock was empty.

Dr. Newman saw him right away. "How's Tito?" he asked, knowing Louis Paul had taken him from the hospital in Gallup against doctor's wishes.

No comment.

"Can I help you, Mr. Jahata?"

"I need to speak to new doctor."

"I have two. Which one?"

"The one who took Tito to hospital."

"That's Jack D'Amico. He isn't here right now. Area Office sent him on a temporary assignment. Sorry, but I can't divulge the location."

"I understand." Louis Paul nodded, turned to leave, but hesitated. "What color are his eyes?"

The question was a left-fielder, but he was accustomed to Louis Paul's point of view. "Blue, very blue. I had an Australian Sheepdog that had blue eyes. China blue, the breeder called them. That dog could lock her gaze on a sheep, control them with the stare, get them to go wherever she wanted. Jack's got eyes like that."

"Thank you."

Louis Paul pulled his dusty brown Ford truck in front of the Tribal Offices. Governor Allen Cooeyate had his sources. A doctor had been sent north to Apache country, to the clinic in Dulce.

"What's wrong, Louis?" asked the governor. "You don't need his help, do you?"

"No."

"My guy said that earthquake shook mountains. Right after doctor got there."

"I know," replied Louis Paul. "*Elahkwa*, Allen."

"You are welcome, anytime. *Don ansammo yadon K'okshi' sunnahk'yanapdu.*"

"I will try to."

Back in Middle Village, Louis Paul closed the door to his workroom. He reached for the crude bear fetish and said out loud, "Blue eyes, you are in great danger."

15

That evening, Lori hefted two sacks of groceries, gave a quick knock at his door and stepped back.

When the light came on in her SUV, Mario realized she was the good-looking girl he had seen earlier at the clinic. So the doctor is having a little hanky-panky on the side. At least that's normal. Something he was very accustomed to himself.

He would have to kill her, too.

Jack opened the door after the second knock, expecting another sick child. He was speechless. She said she was a field nurse, trained in emergency medicine. Jack just stared at her.

"I really didn't know how bad it was up here, but I thought you might need food, so I brought some stuff from Taos," she said. "Well, may I come in?"

He laughed, apologizing for being flustered. "I'm Jack—I've been up to my eyeballs with sick Indians. You surprised me, took my breath away, literally."

She handed him the bags, thinking he was quite the man in his T-shirt, low-slung jeans, and bare feet. She also saw the family resemblance immediately. "The drive was terrible, and I am starving. I make a mean Caesar salad."

"I can't remember when I've had a fresh vegetable—that sounds great. There's no electricity or water yet."

Lori fished around in the grocery bags and pulled out a flashlight. "Can you grill?"

"Am I American, and is this summertime?"

They talked about the earthquake, the epidemic. Indians, the vastness of New Mexico. She ripped the romaine, peeled a clove of garlic and an avocado, whipped an egg. He trimmed and seasoned the steaks. The thought that they were perfect strangers never occurred to either.

Because his father was always at the restaurant, his mother as well in the early days of the business, a maid prepared dinner. That was why

Sunday was his favorite day of the week. He could see them, Pasquale and Rose, side-by-side in the kitchen. Like himself and Lori May Wilson.

"You're good at that," he said.

"Making a salad in the dark?" Lori laughed. "This is nothing—you should see me gut an elk and filet the tenderloin."

"I had too much of that in med school."

Lori grated thin slices of Parmesan over the romaine, then glanced at her watch. "It's getting late. I have a long drive back to Taos."

Jack ignored her, said the charcoal was ready, and stepped out the back door with the steaks. "Bring me another beer, would you? I'll light some candles."

They sat at a small, rusted table. Lori brought out two paper plates heaped with salad. The cracked terrace wasn't level. Jack wedged a match-book under one of the table legs. With a laugh, they agreed they would share the one and only steak knife.

"Here, let me cut your steak. I guess the resident doctor never had any company," said Jack.

"Look what he's missing."

"I never have had time to enjoy the company of a woman, much less a beautiful one."

"You're kidding—I don't believe you."

"I just work—my work is everything. I haven't had much of a private life for the last five years. When you become a doctor, you kind of jump in and never look back."

"I have my work, too, and I'm good at it, but I'm my own woman."

"That suits me fine."

"I'll bet you..."

"Ah, so you're a gambling woman."

"To a degree, let's just say I'm competitive."

"Me, too, my brother and I were at it constantly. One time we..."

Neither of them noticed a man moving from one scrub pine to another, getting closer with every move.

Mario watched. Waited. Part vicarious thrill, part professional killer. Now. Silencer on. He stepped out from behind the piñon with the weapon aimed at Jack.

A shot rang out. A scream filled the air. The bullet buried itself in the ground at the base of the concrete slab.

Jack and Lori jumped back, knocking the table over. His arm flashed out protectively to shield her. From a crouched position, they cringed in horror.

Snarling, growling, bellowing came from a huge brown bear. The first swipe of his enormous claws gouged out the shooter's eyes. A second crushing swipe ripped out the throat. Blood gushed. Arteries pulsed. The bear reared up, screaming defiantly, then vanished.

16

Jack rushed to the mauled body. No heartbeat. The shooter had bled to death. "We've got to get him out of here—that bear might be back."

He half-carried, half-dragged the body inside the house. Lori picked up the revolver, slid it under her shirt at the middle of her back. Jack pointed the flashlight at what was left of the torn carotid artery on the right side.

"I'm going to get Gloria, my nurse. You watch the body."

"No, you're not. I'm with you. This body's going nowhere." She was in Jack's car before him.

Twenty minutes later, Jack and Gloria maneuvered the body on to a stretcher and got it to the clinic. Lori went for the radio. Raised the tribal police. They would contact Fish and Game. Protocol dictated that the bear be tracked and destroyed. Gloria knew Officer Chino and agreed to meet him outside.

In the exam room, Lori said, "I wonder why the bear didn't attack us. We were the ones eating rare steaks."

Jack didn't hear her. He was looking at the gold watch on the dead man's wrist. Exactly like his father's. He aimed the flashlight closer, started to take it off.

"Don't touch him."

"That watch is exactly like my father's."

"There have to be lots of watches like that."

"I've got to look at the back. His initials are engraved on the back. My Mother bought it for him in Venice, on their honeymoon."

Lori placed a vice-like grip on his arm. "Wait for the police." If the watch belonged to Jack's father, she would have to tell him the brutal truth. "I need some air, let's wait outside."

Pacing the exam room, Jack ignored her. Casual but expensive clothes. Soft Italian loafers. Polished fingernails. "What the..."

The waiting room door opened and Gloria appeared, leading a New

Mexico State policeman, dressed in black from head to toe. And a Tribal police officer wearing a baseball cap.

"I heard Officer Chino's radio call. I decided to see what's going on," said the state trooper. "You're the lady that called this in?" Lori nodded. "And you're the replacement doctor?"

Instead of answering, Jack said, "I want to look at the dead man's watch." He took them to the corpse and reached for the limp wrist.

"Hold it, Doc. You're already in trouble for moving the body." The officer pushed Jack back from the table. They all heard the sound of vomiting in the bathroom across the hall. The cop pushed him further from the mauled man. "The body and all items associated with it are property of the State for now. You'll have your turn after the state coroner is finished."

"To hell with that. I am the physician here. Besides, this is not a crime scene."

"I'll decide that. Hey, Paul, get back in here. A bear attack is pretty unusual around here. Not unheard of, but rare, right, Paul?" said the state policeman.

Standing in the doorway, Officer Chino cleared his throat. The heavy-set former Marine said, "First time for me. Seen lots of corpses in Vietnam. This is worst."

"Any of you know him?" asked the cop.

Jack nodded no, as did Gloria and Lori.

Panning the body with a flashlight, Lori said, "His shoes are expensive. Look at the snaffle bit. Gucci. I had a friend in Boston that said you could tell the net worth of a man by his shoes." The light moved to the head. "His face is badly mutilated, but I still think I might have seen him in Gallup a couple of days ago. He was having his shoes shined at El Rancho—I remember the shoes."

"Didn't you say you were from Taos?" Jack interrupted. Watched her body language. "Taos is way east of here. Gallup is southwest."

"I'll explain later, Jack." She pulled her ID folder from her pocket and flashed her badge. "Officers, I'm Special Agent Wilson, Chicago FBI."

"FBI?" asked Officer Chino.

"Yep," said Lori.

Chino stepped back beside Gloria. He knew when to shut up. Fact: a wild animal had killed a White man on Indian land. But the thought of the Feds taking over turned his stomach again.

The state officer looked down at Lori. "You should have ID-ed yourself immediately, but it doesn't matter and you know it. No Federal crime has been committed. This is in my jurisdiction."

Lori started for the door.

"Just a minute," yelled Jack, half-running after her. "Just who the hell are you?"

Lori opened the door of the Scout and reached for the radio mike. Jack reached across her, his hand on the steering wheel. "Does the 'L' really stand for Lori?"

"It does," she said coldly.

"Then why are you here, miles from nowhere?" He didn't let her respond. "Miles from Chicago?" He wanted to smack her, but held back. "Cut the bull, Lori. Are you going to report back like a good girl?"

"Give me some credit. I told you I would explain everything. I'm here to take care of you."

"I'll take goddamned care of myself!"

17

A flat-bed truck carrying the Chevy and the ambulance bearing the body pulled away. The state police cruiser followed, acting as escort to Albuquerque. Lori spoke a few words to Officer Chino before he left with Gloria in tow. Jack watched the vehicles turn onto the highway. The gold watch still on the dead man's wrist. A Cartier, the style of '31. Gone.

He sat down on the front steps. Lori started the Scout. In the dim light, he could see her hand holding the microphone. Who is this woman?

The radio band hissed, crackled as she dialed. Frequency: 170.72500 ChiA3, the primary repeater for the Chicago Field Office. Analog encryption, frequency inversion scrambling assured a secure channel. She refused to talk to anyone except Brooks.

He was on the line surprisingly fast. She heard him dismiss the dispatcher. She relayed the bear attack. The turf battle over jurisdiction. Technically, a Federal law hadn't been violated. She was in the back seat. She got a look at the victim's ID and car registration. Fakes. But she did have something. A Walther PPK. Loaded with special bullets. Hollow nose. Certain to kill.

"The attack was horrendous, so fast; I didn't realize a shot had been fired. I did find the spot where the bullet nicked the concrete deck inches from where Jack was sitting. Must have gone off just as the bear attacked. I'm positive that bullet was meant for him."

"Get it to Albuquerque ballistics. The killer found him. You can be damn sure they'll send someone else when they find out about this. Get Jack out of there. Back to Zuni. And, Agent Wilson, I think it's time that he's told about his family." The connection warbled and spat. "You're breaking up. Brooks, over and out."

Brooks didn't waste any time alerting Admiral Zeller, who updated Dr. Newman. D'Amico was being escorted back to Zuni.

"It's up to you to find somewhere absolutely safe to hide him," said Zeller.

"When will he get here?" asked Bill.

"Three, maybe four hours."

Bill fell back on the bed. Where in hell could he hide the guy?

The pueblo. A person could get lost forever in there. On went the wrinkled chinos and T-shirt left in a pile on the floor.

He had lived on the reservation for three years, long enough to begin to understand the Zunis' relationship between the natural, observable world, and a multitude of supernatural worlds. Ceremonial dances followed the Zuni calendar. Exotic, sometimes grotesque. Mudheads. Kachinas. A Shalako. Kivas were sacred. Secrecy was complete.

Fifteen minutes later, he had driven down to the pueblo, turned left and up the dirt street to the walled cemetery in front of the old mission. The mission, circa 1612, had long dismissed Catholicism. It was home to the Zuni religion.

Across a dusty, weed-and-rock-filled lot to an alley. Walking alone in the pitch black of the moonless night to the sacred plaza. He glanced up. A living maze of mud and stone. Earthen and tin chimney pots. All surreal.

A single naked light bulb glowed in the plaza. He climbed a ladder at midpoint, east side. He knew where to go. He had been summoned once before by Louis Paul Jahata. Old Man Rainbird lay dying atop blankets in the middle of the receiving room. A severe heart attack.

Louis Paul knew his only cardiac medicine, foxglove tea, was weak.

Bill had treated the revered elder. The old man recovered.

He knocked at the low screen door. The door opened immediately. Candles glowed, casting shadows on the hard-packed earthen floor. Smells of piñon smoke, moist wool.

In silence, Louis Paul backed away and sat cross-legged. Hair pulled back in a ponytail. He motioned Bill to join him. Bill outlined his problem, telling him all he knew about Jack D'Amico—and his family.

Louis Paul knew everything he was telling him.

For the first time, he spoke. "I will protect Doctor D'Amico. Bring him to me. Come for him when danger has passed. Good night, Doctor Newman."

Louis Paul sat alone, his mind's eye surveying mountains. Cliff faces. Caves. Hidden places where approaching trails could be watched.

Sacred sites. Kiva members never knew the sites of other kivas. Official Zuni government wasn't involved. Therefore each tribal policeman was only aware of his own kiva. All were sworn to secrecy.

"Yes, I will find a safe place for doctor," he murmured aloud.

18

Lori left the motor idling and slid out of the vehicle. Jack's back was to her as he locked up the clinic.

He swung around, hoping she was going to say 'Adios,' or 'Goodbye, I'm on my way.' Instead, she told him to get in the Scout. "Where are we going?"

"Zuni."

"Zuni, hell. I'm assigned here and there's plenty of mess to clean up, not to mention my sick patients, and the earthquake injuries that are bound to come flooding in."

"Get in."

"Just who the hell do you think you are? You're not going to boss me around."

"Jack, listen, and I mean it, listen to me. People are after you—this very minute. That man was just the beginning, I'm positive. Please, get in."

She shifted into four-wheel-drive when at the detour. Twenty-weeks at Quantico learning driving tactics paid off. Massive boulders. Sheared Ponderosa pines. Sudden drop-offs. Headlights flashed and bounced. Slick clay soil ahead. She slammed the SUV into reverse, gunned it. Whipped the wheel to spin 180-degrees. Like a bucking bronco, she attacked the rock-strewn hillside, skirting the sucking clay pit.

The moon dropped from view, the domed sky went jet-black. Jack turned in his seat to face her. "Exactly what in hell are you doing here?"

Silence.

"Look, it's time." Silence. "It's time to tell me what on earth is going on. Why are you so concerned about me?" Nothing. He slammed his hand on the dashboard.

Her eyes never left the road.

"Shit! What's so goddamned important about me, Miss Lori? Why me?"

"It sure as hell isn't your personality."

He pressed back in his seat, his mind filled with such anger he couldn't think, couldn't speak. Calm down. There had been times in med school when he felt totally without control, completely in over his head. He had thought his way out of each crisis. He was going to think his way out of this one.

Seventy miles an hour. Rock and roll.

"You better slow down—you're going to kill us."

Lori ignored him, pressing down on the gas.

"What the hell is wrong with you?"

Still not a word out of her.

Jack shut his eyes and his mouth. He wanted to stop, bodily pick her up, and get some answers.

Crack. Crack. Smashing violent cracking. A sudden deafening noise. Coming from Lori's side of the road. A wall of rock, earth, and trees were sliding, rolling directly at them. The sound was unbelievably loud. Gathering speed, spewing debris.

"Christ!" he yelled. "The side of the mountain is coming down on us."

Lori shot a glance out her window, only to be met with a mass of rocks striking the hood. She jerked the wheel, pitching them down a precipitous hill toward a wildly rushing stream.

"Can't outrun it!" she yelled over the roar.

The Scout plunged into the churning water. Jack was thrown on top of her. He grabbed the wheel.

"Get your hands off!" yelled Lori.

They were sinking. Submerged. The tires hit bottom. The chassis rotated sideways.

"Hang on." She floored the gas pedal, the wheels spun. They were hit by a torrent of foaming, churning water. Huge branches. Entire tree trunks. Blasting the two-and-a-half ton vehicle, ripping off wipers, cracking the windshield. The rear window imploded. The Scout began a sickening spin.

Completely drenched, Jack sat helpless, watching the frothing water rise toward the base of his window. He grabbed the bar above the door just as one wheel caught on solid ground.

Traction.

She floored the pedal, catapulting the Scout up onto the bank of the rushing creek. A second front wheel grabbed at rock and dirt. The drive train screamed. Traction. The vehicle lurched up and onto the embankment.

The groaning Scout rolled to a stop. Shuddered. The engine died. Jack cranked his window down a few inches. The entire pane dropped into the interior panel. Thunderous sounds bounced and echoed through the canyon. The smell of freshly ripped pine. A metallic taste to the air.

"You did it," he whispered. He touched her shoulder. She jumped.

"Sorry. That was pretty hairy."

"You are one helluva driver."

A half hour passed before Lori attempted to start the engine. It coughed repeatedly, eventually yielded to a rough idle. The mudslide stopped. The convulsed mountainside stilled. Jack wedged out of the Scout, brushed off debris, then picked up a long branch, threaded his way through deep mud and downed trees to the stream and plunged it into the water. About eight inches deep, a slower current. He crawled back up to his seat, mud up to his knees. "Ground clearance good to go."

There was a terrific rattle emitting from the oil pan, so she drove slowly across the Navajo nation toward Gallup. They did not speak. His mind darted, holding a thought was difficult.

Lights came into view. Left on Route 66, to downtown Gallup. They clattered to a stop at a railroad crossing. A shrill whistle of the locomotive. Yellow barriers crashed into place. More than one hundred cars rhythmically thundered on the way to the west coast. Mesmerizing steel wheels sparked the tracks.

In the reflection of flashing red lights, Jack glanced at her. There were tears welling in her eyes. He kept quiet.

At the outskirts of Gallup, the sky lightened to a soft grey. Slight hints of pink warmed clouds to the west. The SUV slowed way down.

"What's wrong? A problem?" he asked.

"Not with the Scout," Lori said, barely audible.

He heard the quiver in her voice. Added to the tears, he was damned worried. Helpless.

He remembered feeling the same inconsolable sense of panic during a particularly difficult home delivery on the south side of Chicago. Fourth year med student at Northwestern. A black bag filled with standard delivery instruments and supplies. A student nurse for backup. Very young mother, labor long, no progress. The unborn baby was in a breach presentation. The baby was born alive. Jack and the student nurse left alive, too. Unnoticed, un-thanked.

Lori pulled onto a rough, narrow shoulder, turned off the engine, head down, hands on the steering wheel. The noise from the dented oil pan ceased. Jack started to open the door, worried about a possible oil leak. She reached for his left arm. Grabbed it with surprising strength. "Don't get out." The quiver was there. "I have to tell you something. Jack...I have to tell you something terrible."

She shifted, looking directly at him. In the pale light, she could see his exhausted eyes, the tension in his face.

Jack braced for whatever she was going to say, feeling not one ounce of the confidence his M.D. gave him.

Holding his forearm tightly, Lori began, "Days ago, in Chicago..."

19

Mr. K sat behind his large barrister desk listening to Mike, his bodyguard. A copper-shaded lamp cast light over the desktop and oriental carpet in the otherwise dark paneled room. The lamp had an engraved plaque on the marble base: *To Anthony Knapp with Great Appreciation—From the Chicago Symphony Orchestra & the Ravinia Festival.* The outline of a figure could be made out seated in one of three wingback chairs.

Mike completed his weekly report. During the fifteen-minute update, Knapp nodded twice.

When he did speak, it was a monotone. "So our man inside the FBI said Mario was killed by a bear?" His voice rose slightly. "A goddamned fucking bear—I'm supposed to believe that? And someone sent his pistol by special delivery for tests, and it had been fired once. Was it the pistol I gave him?"

"My informant didn't say. But D'Amico is still alive."

Knapp stood abruptly, knocking over a brass wastebasket. He kicked the trash can across the rug toward the seated individual. "I can't believe it—Mario blew it. From what you told me, that's not like him."

"We'll get him, sir, I'll do it personally," said the bodyguard.

"No. I need you here. Keep the pressure on your guy downtown."

The man in the wingback rose, intending to leave with Mike. "Where the hell do you think you're going?" hissed Mr. K. "Sit your ass down. The last thing I told you was to hide the new trucks. But, no, all of them are in plain view at the construction site—a government project! Any idiot inspector is going to question ten new rigs. You're just inviting the regulators to check things out."

"I'll take care of it. Don't worry; I know how to keep them off my back."

"You're damn right you will. You're also going to take care of Jack D'Amico yourself. You recommended Mario. Now you do the job!"

Knapp crossed to a credenza. Two inches of single malt Scotch in a cut crystal glass. After a swallow, he slammed the glass down. "Do you realize the Feds probably know the size of your jockey shorts, much less your prick? You get your ass back to the building site and make those goddamn trucks disappear, then pick up Mario's tracks."

A refill of the whisky. Knapp's prematurely grey hair was combed straight back. Exactly like his father and grandfather. He was short, but cut a quietly impressive figure. A preference for double-breasted Dunhill blazers. Custom-made shirts, tailored to fit his barrel chest and thick neck. Half-moon pouches under each eye cast shadows, making them look like he had two black eyes. Gold cufflinks, nothing flashy. He was too smart to want to stand out in a crowd. And no one was going to outsmart him.

The first shipload had arrived from Canada. Already offloaded. Tons of mined rock transported to Gary, Indiana, to Knapp Chemical Processing Co., Inc. Using a combination of acids, uranium-rich ore was impurely separated from the crushed rock. Then packed in steel barrels. Residual rock was packed in thick wooden kegs. These tailings were as radioactive, if not more so, than the semi-pure uranium. This little problem was of no importance to Knapp. Billions to be made. Billions.

He dialed a private long distance number, got right to the point. "Senator, a little something has come up. We may well be exposed."

"Lord, no, Anthony. No way—I am not to be involved."

"Get that damn bill on the floor tomorrow. It sure as hell has been in committee a long time." Knapp hesitated to allow the senator to do a bit of mathematics. If he didn't get that property re-aligned so it was designated as federal land, they both could lose millions.

He told him a shipment was going out right away, adding softly, almost whispering, "Joseph, you do understand what could happen if someone stumbles on to those trucks, don't you?"

20

With one hand rolled in Josh's FBI vest, Lori tried to sweep the broken glass from the dashboard and seats. Sunlight raked over the cliff face, glinting off the glass shards, flashing in her eyes. She looked through the shattered windshield to see Jack emerge from the dark forest at the base of the cliff. He walked slowly past an old wooden corral and loading chute, and back uphill to the Scout. He had been gone for nearly an hour, one of the longest hours in her life.

At one point she heard a horrible sound. Like a dying animal. She could only guess what he was going through. A crushing, disintegrating hurt.

Eyes averted, he struggled with the mangled door. His knuckles were bleeding, like a fighter. He wrapped his arms around his chest. Visibly shuddered. Head down, he murmured, "Let's go, I've got a lot to do."

She didn't reply, knowing plans were in place for him. She needed help to explain the next move, a decision made without his input. Driving as fast as the Scout would allow, she made it to the hospital emergency entrance at Black Rock.

"What are you doing? I'm not going in there! Take me to my Jeep, down the street. I'm catching the first flight to Chicago."

"You need to see Doctor Newman first, then you can do whatever you want. Remember, you're in the military, I believe with the equivalent rank of Navy Lieutenant. Am I correct?"

He felt a choking in his throat. His heartbeat was deafening. He hit the jammed door with his shoulder, kicked glass out of the way, slid out. Jerked the ER door open, letting it slam behind him. Lori ran after him, praying Bill Newman was ready.

He was. He wrapped an arm around Jack's shoulders, guided him into his office. "I'm so sorry. I really feel for you."

Jack pulled back, his jaw set. He looked feverish, his muddy shirt was stained with sweat. He smelled of grief. He stared at Bill, said flatly, "Feel what? I missed the goddamned funeral! But, I'm sure you know that."

He wanted to call him a bastard, a liar, but held back. "I have to go home. At least I can see my family's graves."

"It's too dangerous, Jack. Zeller gave me direct orders to hide you until things are safe. We've got to protect you, all of us do. We're the good guys."

"Then why doesn't it feel like it?" A vein in his neck pulsated; he swung around, looking menacingly at Lori. "You've been flat-ass lying to me from the get-go. The nice little dinner you showed up with. How did you know where to find me?"

"I told Doctor Newman we were engaged. That I wanted to surprise you." Her speech dropped to a bare whisper. Tears welled in her eyes and spilled over.

"I understand you want to strike out at someone, at both of us," Bill said. "But you've got to understand one helluva a lot of people are working for you."

"Working for me?" His mind couldn't grasp what Bill was saying. His entire family had been wiped out. A singularly horrendous fact. "Bill, I know Chicago, I can take care of myself. I can handle anything that comes my way."

"I'm sure you think you can, but..."

"I said I can, didn't you hear me? I'm going home, end of discussion. I need to honor them." He started for the door.

"You shall do as you are ordered, or I will..."

"You'll what? There's not much you can do to hurt me."

"I will have you locked up for disobeying a direct order."

"You think so?"

Bill called out, "Gentlemen, come in."

Stan and two tribal policemen entered the office. "Don't make me do it, Jack," said Bill. "Whoever is after you must be big time, very big time. Let the professionals do their job."

"Well now, just what do you have planned for me?"

Bill explained how people could disappear in the pueblo. He had gone to Louis Paul. "He didn't hesitate. He feels completely indebted to you for saving his son, Tito."

His back to everyone, Jack stared at the surface of his desk. A stack of charts waited for his signature. Beside them was the envelope Gabriel D'Amico had handed to him before he left home. HOME. Too fatigued from the overwhelming drain, he acquiesced. "What's next?"

Lori wiped her eyes. Bill took a deep breath. Both of them were fighting to contain their own emotions, knowing there was space for only one broken person in the room.

"The tribal police will drive you to the Middle Village. They will escort you to Mr. Jahata," said Bill. "I'll watch your back."

"Me, too," Lori said in a whisper.

Dressed in a short-sleeved plaid shirt, jeans with a leather belt and large silver buckle, Tito greeted Jack. "Welcome to our home, Doctor." No cast, no bandage, nothing but residual redness on his arm. He knew what Jack was thinking. Flexed his bicep. "Almost well."

"*Keshi*, welcome, Doctor D'Amico, to *Halona Idiwan'a*, home of the *A:shiwi*," said Louis Paul. He took a step back, smoothing his shoulder-length hair. "Your actions saved him."

"His arm..."

"I'll tell you what I've planned for you. First, eat."

Eating was the last thing Jack cared about, but he followed them to a table prepared for one. Bowl. Spoon. Hesitation.

Louis Paul noticed. "*Chuleya:we*, Zuni stew—it will help."

A short woman wearing a needlepoint turquoise necklace over a purple blouse appeared. Long hair pulled into a knot. High cheekbones, slanted eyes. She placed a black iron kettle, wooden ladle in front of him. Even without the pork pie hat, she knew he recognized her.

"My wife, Linda."

"We've met." She liked to wash Dr. Bill's dishes with a hose.

"Her primary clan is Bear, her secondary clan is Dogwood. From the Crow," said Louis Paul. "I am from the Tobacco clan, secondary is Badger. I tell you this, Doctor, because all Zuni children are schooled in their heritage. No intermarriage of bloodlines."

Zuni bloodlines were not intermixed. Not within the pueblo. Not with other tribes. Zuni blood is pure.

"Ah, he gets it," said Linda. "He might understand how we live the Zuni way. And cook," she added with a crinkled smile.

Louis Paul removed the lid, releasing the smell of braised mutton. Simmering in golden-red broth. He filled the bowl. "*Idonapshe*, eat,"

Jack took a spoonful. Chunks of lamb, potatoes, carrots. And fire.

"*Chuleya:we*. Special. Make you strong," said Tito. "Father's recipe the best."

An image of his own father popped into Jack's mind. Like a kaleidoscope, images flashed so fast he thought his brain would explode. He closed his eyes tightly. Exhaled.

Louis Paul felt Jack's breath touch his own face. He opened his mind, joining Jack's. Pervasive grief. He understood the man's excruciating sadness. "Eat. Then we talk."

Later Jack found himself sitting between Tito and Louis Paul in an old Ford truck, barreling down a corrugated dirt road. Tito drove, spewing gravel and a cloud of dust behind them.

He remembered eating the stew. All of it. Dribbling some. Fry bread to mop up the broth. No talk. Mysterious calm. Alert. Clear-headed. Powerful. No anger, no angst.

Chuleya:we gave him more than just strength.

It had given him peace.

Tito turned off the road, down-shifted. The Ford groaned up the steep incline. Crowned out, wove between piñon, junipers, down into a grove of giant cottonwoods. Low branches scraped the cab. Dappled light pierced the shade, highlighting new growth of the chamisa. Within view of a wind-carved butte, the engine coughed to a stop. A mourning dove cooed. Quiet.

They all climbed out of the truck to face the cliff. Louis Paul stepped in front of Jack and placed both hands on his shoulders. He looked inside Jack, concentrating his thoughts, aligning him with life spirit. He did not speak, but silently called upon everything in the universe—natural forces such as lightning, wind, great droughts, to physical entities like rocks, animals, rivers, and humans—to permeate the man before him with the universal spirit *Isa-ha-i*. He intended to link Jack with the entirety of nature and the cosmos, the life force in all beings.

He said out loud, "This is far as I go. Special cave up there. Hide. Snake god will protect. I pray for you. Tito will go between. Go."

Jack knew the man was going to take care of him.

Tito led. Up, down red arroyos. Daylight was failing. Jack finally could make out the entrance to the cave, thirty feet from the top. They stopped.

The cliff. Sheets of pure granite. Crevices. Precipitous cleavages. Eons of exposure to wind, ice.

"Do not let negative thoughts bother you." Tito handed Jack a small leather pouch. "Snake fetish, keep it. Always."

With a basket strapped to his back, Tito slunk up like a lizard. Fast. Like a blur. He disappeared into the rock.

Jack hesitated. A giant cast shadow swallowed the canyon. A single sheet of darkness engulfed him. Suddenly, he was sitting cross-legged at the cave entrance. Sitting on a finely woven Indian horse blanket.

"I must go. The light," said Tito softly.

"What about water?"

"A spring, back of cave."

"What time will you be back? What's the schedule?"

"No schedule. There is no time in Zuni," Tito said.

21

At his desk, speaking to Admiral Zeller, Bill said, "Yes, sir, he's taken care of." He hung up and covered his mouth and a big yawn.

"Doctor Newman," said the head nurse. "Mr. Jahata is here to see you."

"Good, send him in right away."

Louis Paul said only, "The doctor is safe. You may use your powers to keep him that way," and left.

Bill touched the fetish he always kept in his pocket. He had been secretly honored by the Zunis. He had been inducted into the rattlesnake fraternity.

The extremely surreal experience began in a kiva, a big round gathering house, painted floor-to-ceiling with god figures, winged monsters, mythical animals with grotesque masks. All the images in the murals were winding in and out of giant corn plants in iconographic chaos. Men were singing. Loud and harmonious. Overwhelming.

He was escorted to an altar at the distant side of the acrid-smelling room. The attendants at the altar, all smoking cigarettes, sat around a blazing fire nearby. All the men were nude, their painted bodies covered entirely with symbols Bill didn't understand. Hands, heads and feet were striped red, yellow and white.

At first glance, he thought the men were wearing skin-tight garments, until he was stripped, and at each stage of the ceremony, painted with another symbolic image. At one point --- he couldn't recall when because he was so disoriented—someone handed him a crude cigarette. With one draw, he became nauseated, but the sensation quickly faded. A strong sense of calm settled within.

He didn't mind the rattlesnakes draped around his neck, their exposed fangs inches from his face and bare chest. All he felt was the intense chill of the subterranean chamber and the pounding of his heart. He was given a snake fetish and asked to close it in his hand. During the chants that followed, he didn't even notice that the snakes had slithered off his body.

At the conclusion, he was told of the power and protection he now possessed, courtesy of his fellow brethren, the rattlesnake. Furthermore, he was told at his will he could use his power to protect others.

They were believers. Expression of belief astonishing. What did they believe in? Bears? Nature? He was knocked out by it all. He believed it, too. He did not have to know.

Bill asked Stan to take a look at the battered Scout. Lori grabbed a duffle from the back seat and fell into step with Bill. They crossed the street to his house where they were greeted by Flipper.

"I have two guestrooms—take your pick. Got to check on my very p.g. dog first. This big guy is the father."

Lori dropped her bag on the floor and followed Bill to the garage, shutting the door behind her. Bill squatted beside a very tired new mother. Flapper had delivered by herself, five new puppies. Eyes still closed, they were sleeping beside her, snuggling against her side, burrowed in the blankets.

Bill soothed the Newfoundland, praising her work and smiled up at Lori. "Delivering babies is my specialty and she didn't need me at all. Oh, I almost forgot to ask you. How's your pregnancy going?"

Lori laughed. "You believed me."

"A woman's prerogative," Bill chuckled. He left to get a batch of clean towels, fresh water and kibble.

Later Lori took a shower while Bill fixed ham and cheese sandwiches, and opened two beers. When she didn't appear, he knocked quietly on her door. She was dressed in an oversized white T-shirt, with a towel wrapped around her head, in deep sleep on the single bed. He ate both sandwiches, drank both beers and crashed.

"What are you doing up so early? Did you sleep okay?" asked Bill, exhausted from a night dealing with an accident at the junction of Route 4 and NM-602. A semi-truck trailer T-boned a van loaded with hippies. "They called me at two AM—hope it didn't wake you. I can hardly think."

"Nothing could have awakened me. I raided your frig for breakfast and took care of Mom and the pups."

"Thank you." He poured two cups of coffee from a pot in the corner.

"What do you know about Jack?"

"He's in Jahata's hands, who's a very powerful man in the tribe, a shiwani. That's all I know."

"You mean you don't actually know where he is?"

"No. If someone like me, his colleague, knew where he was, I suppose I'd pretty soon be dead meat."

Lori sat down at Jack's desk and told him that the mauled corpse was in Albuquerque for autopsy. The case had somehow been shifted to the jurisdiction of the FBI.

She tapped the desktop with her fingertips, finally saying, only because she needed his help, "I found the pistol the man was carrying. I had ballistics check it out, they sent it on to Chicago. I had the strange feeling from the start that I had seen the guy before, maybe a mug shot, but I wasn't sure. He turns out to be a known contract killer. Based in Chicago. Associated with big shots. I'm surmising the latter because the DC office has suddenly taken an interest in the case. If Washington is interested, this is a big deal, and I need to know where Jack is, right now."

Bill, whose fatigue had temporarily vanished, replied, "I don't know where he is. But if Washington is interested, I may know why. I'm going to tell you something super-secret. You probably won't believe me."

"Try me. Since I got to New Mexico, damn little surprises me anymore." She walked to the one window in the office, and with her back to Bill, said, "Shoot."

With a sense of anxiety in his voice, Bill told her that a number of years before arriving in Zuni, there had been an epidemic of lung cancer. "Also a pot full of tragic genetic defects in newborns."

Most of the victims were from the north and west portions of the reservation, areas adjoining the Navajo reservation. The federal government sent investigators, but no official report was ever distributed to the on-site doctors. Rumors around the rez said it originated with the mining of large uranium deposits on leased reservation land.

"I had a good friend, a physics wiz at Los Alamos labs, look into it. He sent me as much info as he could relating to radiation. In short, wherever you find uranium, you'll also find decay products, one of which is radium. In turn, that radium gradually disintegrates into radon gas. Actually, a group of radon progeny. The bottom line, Lori, is that all these products are dangerously radioactive, and are breathed in by the people working the mines."

Lori turned to look at him. "Didn't the Fed do something about it?"

"Only after one helluva battle. I testified before Congress. I supplied a lot of the patient data—got my butt whacked good by Area Office for doing it." He told her that in the early 1950's, under the protective umbrella of the Department of Labor, and the Small Business Administration, Mom-and-Pop uranium shaft miner outfits were encouraged to operate on Indian land. With the blessing of the Atomic Energy Commission, the Bureau of Indian Affairs not only participated, but encouraged the leases. At least two-hundred loans were made by the SBA to uranium exploration companies in the name of economic development.

"Nothing—nada—was ever said about the risks of uranium-bearing ore, though I know full well there were written reports documenting the dangers buried somewhere in Washington.

With an edge to his voice, Bill continued, his outrage obvious. "The Indians lost a huge amount of land to contracts made between the government and several big industrial outfits who wanted to mine on reservation land. There was overt confiscation of herds of Indian-owned sheep and cattle, leaving the Native Americans destitute. They shipped them to Gallup for sale, but some of the animals were herded into corrals and just left to starve to death. Poor devils," Bill said. "Thank God that's all stopped. It's one reason I've stayed in Zuni."

He refilled both their cups. "There's something else I want to tell you that is still a mystery to me. I've never told anyone. As thanks for my testimony, I was inducted into one of the kiva fraternities—the Rattlesnake."

"I suppose that's quite an honor," she said, a trace of skepticism in her voice.

"It carries a great personal power. I was told I can transfer this power to someone in need. For what it's worth, at dawn, I prayed that the powers of the rattlesnake be with Jack."

"Okay, I'll buy into your story, despite the fact I don't trust anything without shoulders." But what did that have to do with Jack? Uranium? Radium poisoning in New Mexico. Mass murder in Chicago. "I've got to get to Jack."

"Jahata was just here, I'll take you to him. If he chooses to tell you, then you're in."

◈ ◈ ◈

Jack awoke to complete silence. He had curled into a tight ball, holding his ankles tightly to keep from falling off the ledge. Pale light filtered through low clouds, the new moon resonated high above. He scooted back, stretched his stiff legs, his hand touching the basket Tito had left. He picked up the smell of smoke; smoke unique to Tito's mother's cookstove.

Three jars of stew. Three apples. A bag of some sort of seeds. Dried corn. Flashlight. Cup, spoon. A mirror.

He was thirsty. Knowing he had to conserve the batteries, he flashed the light briefly, then allowed his eyes to adjust to the darkness. An off-shoot to the right. Stay in the main gallery. Tito warned of sink holes. Rock tore his knees. The ceiling was too low to stand. Suddenly a loud rattling sound came from ahead. He turned on the flashlight. The corridor appeared to widen. He slowly moved forward. Stopped abruptly by a very active rattle. He turned off the light, afraid the snake would attack. Staying absolutely still, the only sound he could hear was his own heart beating. The rattling stopped, and he could hear a slithering sound which (thank God) slowly disappeared further into the darkness.

He was sweating despite the coolness in the dank channel. Flashlight on. No snake in sight. He edged forward, inch by inch, but stopped when his lead hand felt no rock, only space. Directing the flashlight downward, he realized he was at the edge of a chasm. Sheer sides of a black bottomless pit plunged downward, with no floor in sight. His breathing was shallow, his palms wet. He noticed a narrow natural bridge to his right. He carefully crossed the six-foot gap, and in the narrow field of the flashlight, he saw something shining.

"Water—it's the pool." He was shocked to hear his voice. Cupping his hand, he tasted the water. Fresh spring water. Sweet, icy cold. He sat back on his haunches and splashed the freezing water on his face, realizing the snake had warned him, saving him from certain death. He fingered the fetish Tito had given him, then pressed it to his wet lips.

Bill preceded her up the ladder. Left her at the screen door. Louis Paul rose to greet her, his head silhouetted against a small square window. The room smelled old. Not musty. Old. Austere. Very austere. Only essentials. A kiva fireplace in the northeast corner. Neatly stacked piñon wood. A broom. Rocking chair. One goatskin. A profound stillness.

She noted surface electrical wiring, a bulky metal switch box—not recessed. Connected to a single overhead fixture. A naked light bulb. The black, wall-mounted telephone looked out of place. The sound of a radio commentator speaking in Zuni filtered into the room, followed by static. Someone turned it off.

Silence again. She had been in seamy, sleazy bars, filthy ghettos, third-world diarrhea-ridden barrios, surrounded by men from the dregs of the earth, but walking into Louis Paul's primitive home unsettled her more than any place she had ever been. He seemed polite, yet a certain invisible unknown, an unseen power touched the very core of her being.

She felt as if she had lost control. Not physically, but mentally. She was not uncomfortable. A strange feeling, something she had never experienced, even when enduring a mind-altering drug exercise during training. She was prepared to deal with capture and truth serums, brainwashing and torture.

This was different.

She began quietly, explaining that she was the agent in charge of Dr. D'Amico's case. "I desperately need to find him. I have many important questions; Jack might have the answers. I promise you that I am on his side."

Louis Paul appeared to ignore her for a long while, silently considering his own promise. He remained silent as she pulled the rocking chair closer to him and sat down, her hands draped casually over the wooden arms. Her eyes fixed on his. When she shifted in her seat, rocking ever-so-slightly, he remained still, his expression revealing nothing.

Finally, he walked to his work bench in the niche, picked up a small mirror.

"Are you strong?" he asked.

"Very."

"Go as sun rises. Face the sun. Look high. Signal him. Careful. Others may watch you."

22

Impenetrable blackness. He closed his eyes, but there was no difference than with his eyes wide open. His ears buzzed, he needed to pee. Indigo. Deep purple. He thought he could see a faint light at the four-foot wide, four-foot high mouth of the cave. He shrugged off the blanket. Another sleepless night over.

In all of his years of medical training, sleep had come instantly. However, the sound of a bedside phone would awaken him immediately. Completely alert. Ninety-six hours since the night of the bear attack and the insane drive back to Zuni. Seventy-two hours since Lori had told him about the murders. The annihilation of his family.

He seemed to breathe slower, as if living in another body rhythm, like a hibernating bear. His heart rate had slowed, (he checked it repeatedly). Down to thirty-eight. Normally seventy-two. Mysterious calm, that's what he called it. No sleep, yet he was extremely alert.

He splashed water from a mason jar onto his face. He pocketed the last jar of stew, crawled toward the light, stood erect on the narrow ledge. He stretched, pulling in the warmth of the sun. His dilated eyes stung. He shut them tightly. His mind was completely clear, like the cool water at the back of the cave.

He pulled off his shirt and tilted his head back. As he looked up at the sky, a black object hurtled toward the ground, streaking by the ledge by no more than a foot. He was not afraid. Watching intently, he saw the object grab a darting dove on the canyon floor. He could see it clearly as if he had binoculars. The giant bird skillfully swept away from the cliff with its prey, spreading broad blue-black wings, soaring out of sight.

He had never seen such a death executed so quickly and efficiently.

He shook the kill from his mind. He was ready for a little risk, confident he would not fall. Distance from the cave to the top of the cliff was about thirty feet. Everything shimmered in the heat waves. A wind-tortured juniper growing in sienna veins jutted out about five feet above the ledge.

He got a foothold on a two-inch outcropping and sprung for the juniper branch. It held.

He was at the top in minutes. He pulled himself to the rim, lunged over the edge and crawled to rest against the bleached trunk of a fallen alligator juniper.

The wind was stronger at the top; he planted his feet solidly beneath him. By the position of the sun, he oriented his body to face north where he mentally envisioned the pueblo. He held his arms out, aligned east and west, imprinting each change of terrain to a map in his brain. Every landmark became part of a three-dimensional screen inside his head—a topographic screen he could move through, coursing back and forth. Over and under. Fast or slow.

He closed his eyes and leaned into the wind. His heart rate accelerated, his eyes flooded with tears. He screamed the names of his family into the wind. The words ricocheted out in an explosive burst of anguish.

Rose.

Pasquale.

Tristina.

Giovana.

Nic.

Jo Lou.

Wooly.

The velocity of the wind increased, whistling as it struck the sandstone bluff. He opened his eyes. The sun blinded him, his knees gave way. He collapsed to the hard ground.

23

Jack was out cold. No motion. No mentation. The only part of his being, his heart, pounded on. Ever-so-slowly his mind acknowledged and recognized the heartbeats. The regularity, the increasing intensity. Pounding. Pounding.

Horses hooves. Clydesdales. The parade. Milwaukee. Dad and Mother gathering all of us in front of them as bands marched by. Giant horses drawing a huge wagon. The street lined with laughing spectators. Children jumping up and down at the sight of clowns on stilts passing out balloons. An anniversary parade sponsored by Anheuser-Busch. A circus, carnival rides. Hot dogs, soft drinks. Cotton candy.

"Get your cotton candy! Fresh, yummy cotton candy!" called a vendor.

"Can we?" asked Nic. Pasquale nodded.

"I'll stay with the girls and Jo Lou," said Rose, smiling down at the twins in the double pram.

Jack and Nic were already running through the falling leaves toward the white-clad man hawking the pink clouds of spun sugar. Pasquale close behind.

Jack was mesmerized. Completely mesmerized.

The man grasped the cone at the narrow end between two fingers and his thumb, broke into the web of floss near the spinner head, and picked up a starter of melted sugar. With a lightning-flash motion, he lifted the cone out of the pan, wrapping the floss in a figure-eight spin, creating a giant air pocket. He presented the diaphanous pink cloud to the smaller, ten-year-old, wide-eyed Jack.

A wintery blast of wind gusted down the street, picked up the translucent cloud of spun sugar, dropping it directly on Nic's head. The gauzy pink mass was plastered on his head. Sticky sweet strands stuck like glue to his thick black hair.

Everyone laughed.

The wind whistled more intensely, striking the sandstone bluff.

Milwaukee faded. The music stopped. The cotton candy gone. His family vanished. Jack was alone.

24

Late afternoon. Thunderheads developed, white towers against cobalt sky. His perch on the ledge was gradually being engulfed in shadow. The rocky surface was still hot to the touch. Then a cool breeze and the smell of rain.

He was hungry. Also edgy, nervous. Ready to pounce, to attack. By his watch, it was nearly six o'clock. He didn't see the figure approach the east-oriented cliff. But he heard the scraping sound. He spotted the top of Tito's head. Black hair tied in a chango knot with red cloth.

"God, am I glad to see you."

"*Keshshi!* Hungry?" Tito said, pushing a canvas bag toward him.

"Tell me what's going on. How soon can I get out of here?"

Tito, unlike his father, was somewhat informative. "My Father has ways of finding out things. He trusts FBI woman. He thinks it is unusual to be out here by herself, but she is a top agent. Tops in her class at their training center. Sharp shooter. Self-defense. She was at the funeral for your family. She wants to ask you questions." A rare smile. "And, she's single."

"When do I meet up with her? Or Bill, or your father? Someone has to tell me what's going on, and why I'm in hiding." He scratched his developing beard. "I'm going crazy—I've got to get out here." He had asked these questions before. No answer. In frustration he said, "Look, Tito, I owe my family. I have things to finish."

"We know that. You will leave at the right time."

"And when the hell will that be? Tomorrow at six o'clock, or twenty-fours, a week, a month?"

"We don't talk like you. We say 'by planting time,' or 'in four moons.' It is now Orion, our warrior in the east; this is your June. Do not rush my Father."

"Your father is a very important man, right? Very wise." Tito nodded. "I respect that. Can you tell me what he does, what is his title, or position? I want to know."

"Hard to say in words. Especially to a non-Zuni. He is a mediator between human and spirit worlds. I know he can visit the Inner World. He can call on spiritual helpers from Unseen World for guidance. Everything in our universe comes from *A'wonawil'ona*. All creations, including Life Spirit, links humans with all of Nature and the Cosmos. We are one with animals, plants, even rocks under our feet."

"But rocks are inanimate objects," said Jack.

"Their power is dormant. Remember Nature. It will teach you. This rock," he said, tapping his boot on a boulder. "This rock has a spirit like a hibernating bear, or a seed that has not been planted. That is why we believe in fetishes." He removed a small turquoise fetish of an eagle from his shirt pocket. Held it in his hand. "I am now touched by the spirit and power of this bird. When you understand the eagle spirit, you understand your connection with spiritual web that moves through all. With work and prayer, I can share the eagle's ability to soar high, to see even the tiniest movements below."

Jack nervously changed position. "Early this morning I saw something that blew my mind. I've never seen a bird so fast."

"Describe it."

"It looked like an oil droplet from a distance; closer, it was like a sleek, black rocket streaking toward the ground. It made a quick kill, soared up, turned, disappeared."

"A falcon. Common here. The perfect predator." Tito explained how the bird could pull up to twenty-five G's in a fast climb, way more than any human pilot could endure. A falcon, particularly peregrine falcons, can fly two-thousand feet above ground.

Tito was gesturing more than usual, his diction more precise. "Peregrines are the fastest animal on the planet. Capable of diving at speeds of two-hundred, maybe two-hundred-and-sixty miles an hour. Baffles in their nostrils keep their lungs from bursting—like jet engines. Their field of vision is peripheral, but, unlike humans..."

Jack interrupted, "Fastest animal on the planet? How do you know all this?"

"I want to be a pilot."

"You sound like you have flown."

"Not yet."

"I climbed to the top this morning. I can't explain it, but I felt like I had a compass in my head that would tell me where I needed to go."

"It is possible. Learn from Nature. Falcons choose selective targets. Nothing random."

Just like his family, Jack thought.

Tito slid over the side, locking in a foot hold. "Watch the ground tomorrow."

25

Late afternoon. Lori borrowed Bill's van, transferred her gear. She had to get back to Gallup.

When she stopped at the desk to get her key, the receptionist handed her a sealed envelope. She retreated to a darkened corner of the lobby by the staircase. Turning her back, she read the typed note telling her to go to a public phone and call Brooks' office ASAP.

Yolanda picked up on the first ring. "You need to know more. I'm sending intel by courier. Be at Coal and First Street at nine forty-five." The line went dead. She had ten minutes to get there.

In the shadows of a side street, she canvassed the store fronts. Under the halo of a street light, she saw a trading post on the corner. Locals taking in pawn. Men—Zunis, Hopis, Navajos—stood outside the entrance of a bar, all staring at the ground, waiting for a magic bottle of Thunderbird wine to appear from the cracked sidewalk. She stayed in the shadows by a dead tree, listening to the pulsating rhythm of a train passing through downtown. Taillights heading east and west. The air smelled of stale beer, cigarettes. Urine. A car backfired. A hand touched her shoulder, pushing her aside. The Indian was drunk. She sidestepped as he fell to his knees and wretched, vomiting strings of spittle. She held her breath, pushed back a strand of hair. Steeled herself to walk to the corner. The sound of the train blasting down the tracks diminished. A full moon emerged from behind a dark cloud bank silhouetting a thin dirty cat in front of her just before it scampered between her legs.

A grey-haired man in baggy jeans and a polo shirt limped toward her and said, "Know a good place to stay? I'm lost and it's pretty grungy around here." Josh Flores. He partially opened a folded map, held it up, obscuring their faces.

Lori felt the envelope in the map and slipped it into her blouse. He thanked her loudly, limped away. She went inside the trading post, squinting in the fluorescent light, bought some postcards, and slid the envelope in the bag.

She took a zigzag route back to the hotel. No one followed.

The unmarked envelope contained five pages of single-spaced intel. Twenty minutes and two read-throughs, her mind was on fire, her hands ice cold. Words like *radioactivity, shipments, senators, top bosses in Chicago's criminal world.*

At the end of the list, Yolanda's cursive writing warned: *Be discreet, remain obtuse when asked about Mr. Blue Eyes. More when I can. Yolie.*

She was hungry and needed a drink. She took a shower, slipped on a navy shirt and white shorts, went down to the bar. A club sandwich and a double bourbon, water on the side. Two cowboy types tried to check her out, asked her to join them. She really didn't know why they were hitting on her—she was poorly dressed, no makeup, and her red lacquered fingernails were a wreck. Smoothly fending the fellows off, though one was rather attractive, she left most of the sandwich and downed her drink.

Walking upstairs, her peripheral vision registered something wrong. A well-dressed, older man was sitting in the lobby, reading a newspaper. She had last seen him at the D'Amico funeral—he was Jack's uncle, Gabriel. She ran up the stairs two at a time.

What was Gabriel D'Amico doing in Gallup? Did Brooks know Gabriel had left Chicago? She didn't trust the telephone. Neither did Yolanda.

She sat on the edge of the bed in her darkened room. Where are the connections, and why is Jack involved?

Thunder rolled. Tumbled, growled. Rolled again. Bill went to his office window, looking between the venetian blinds. Brilliant flashes in the distance. He could smell rain. It was nearly midnight, time to quit. In the light of the single gooseneck lamp, he glanced down at his calendar. That was when the hair on the back of his neck bristled. He looked up.

The stranger's face was cobalt blue against the darkness of the room. The man was well-dressed, down to his shiny laced brogues.

"What can I do for you? Is there an emergency?" asked Bill. "I'll call..."

"No. Don't call anyone. I'm here to see you." Without extending his hand, he said, "I'm Jack's uncle, Gabriel D'Amico."

"You're here to see him?"

"Of course, didn't he tell you I was coming?"

"No, he didn't. I didn't even know he had an uncle. Are you from Chicago as well?" Suspicion was obvious in Bill's voice. He didn't care.

Gabe sat down. Bill remained standing. "Yes. Has Jack told you much about his family?"

"No, not really. He said his father has a restaurant. He didn't mention you."

"Well, when he left home in the middle of the night, not even saying goodbye, I got worried. His mother isn't well, a bad bout of asthma. My brother had to take her to a specialist in Canada."

"That explains things." No way. Not one thing matches Zeller's report.

"What do you mean?"

"Jack's been unable to reach his family." Bill relaxed a little. "I'll tell him. It will make him stop worrying."

"I'll tell him myself." His eyes glistened in the subdued light. "Also, I brought something for him."

"He's away right now."

"When do you expect him back?"

"Don't really know, my boss didn't say."

"Then where is he? I want to tell him about Rose."

"I don't know where he is, sir. I wasn't told. Military rules. I don't ask questions."

Gabriel D'Amico stood up, his expression cold. "Once more, Doctor Newman, where's Jack? I'll be back in the morning. I suggest you refresh your memory."

Bill paced the office. Why did that bastard lie? If he really was Jack's uncle, why didn't he know about the murders? He looked at his watch. Only a few hours until the piece of shit would be back.

26

*B*efore daybreak she dressed in a short-sleeved shirt, cargo pants, hiking boots. FBI badge in her pocket. A denim work shirt hid her Bureau revolver. Mirror in her backpack. She took the housekeeping stairs, walked briskly back toward the side street where she had left the van.

Drunks sleeping off binges were still out cold, sprawled, curled, or propped up in alleys. A woman looked up at her with dead eyes, then rolled back into her cardboard shelter. A small hand appeared from the darkened box, palm up. Lori folded a ten, pressed the bill into the child's hand. The little boy's eyes were huge, his expression blank.

As she drove away she wondered where the money would go. Food or booze? Approaching the pueblo, the light was flat, grey upon grey with no warmth. She scanned the surrounding cliffs. Louis Paul said she should face the new day. East-facing cliffs. Also sheltered. On high. Defendable. She was about to turn back to Black Rock when she spotted several cliffs south of the road, all facing east. She left the road, dipping down to a non-maintained dirt road. Very quickly the road disappeared, turning into a single track. She would have to hike.

Glancing at the glimmer of sun, she set a course paralleling the cliffs, so she could angle the mirror to catch the light. Anyone watching would see flashes. Maybe signal back.

Suddenly the grey vanished, warm light spread around her. Slipped on sunglasses. It took her an hour and thirty minutes to reach the second, and highest, cliff. She was in superb shape. Climbed most of the 14ers in Colorado by the time she graduated. Still, she had to stop to get her breath, mainly because of the heat. As a freshman and sophomore, she couldn't afford a car, so she bicycled around campus, packing in a nineteen-hour academic load and working in the canteen on weekends. Not that she didn't party, but soon tired of flat-assed drunk frat boys passing out on derelict couches lined on the front porches of Boulder's collegiate hangouts. A stint waitressing at the Catacombs got her enough money to buy a used Jeep which could access every base trail in the state.

Prickly burrs clung to her. She set the mirror on a boulder, rolled down her sleeves, pulled her hair into a knot, and wrapped a bandana around her forehead. The mirror caught sunrays. She swung to her right, mentally tracking the line of sight from her position to the cliff.

Nothing but the sound of a male quail calling out. She was close enough to see his curved black crown.

She continued to climb horizontally, grabbing thick blue gramma grass for a hold. Three hours passed. She was sweated out. Decided to give up when she hit a patch of thick, ropy pahoehoe lava. The dark, glassy surface was extremely rough and jagged. Disgusted with herself, she wondered if her hunch was wrong. She gave herself fifteen minutes of rest. Intrigued with the lava, she tapped the butt of her weapon on the surface. Rapped again. Harder. Harder. Realized the thickness of the crust was thin. A foot deep or less. She carefully lifted herself up and around the flow. Shifted her body to stabilize herself. Slipped. Lava rock ripped at her body. Tearing her shirt, her hands. It happened so fast she didn't even have time to make a defensive move to protect her face. Sunglasses went flying.

A tenacious piñon clinging to the cliff face stopped the fall. Jutting precariously at a right angle, she was able to snag a hold with one leg on the trunk. Damage assessment. Shredded skin on both hands. Nasty slash under her chin. Bleeding, but she knew facial cuts do that. Her cargo pants were torn. Bloody knees. But she could climb. She checked her backpack for the mirror.

A flash, though fleeting, came from up high. She quickly adjusted her focus with the mirror on the uppermost terrain.

Another flash, then another.

Looking above, she could see horizontal stratas disappear into a fissure, a rupture with a small opening, barely high enough to stand. Standing on the horizontal tree trunk, she swung a leg up and over the edge. Straining, praying the roots would hold, she pulled her torso up. Up. Up. Breathe. Up again. Her cheek rested on cool rock.

A barely audible sound came from the blackness beyond the opening. Scratching. No—it was scraping. She struggled to her bloody knees, looked up into the bearded face of a man with two searing blue pinholes in sunken eye sockets.

"Jack?"

◈ ◈ ◈

Tito was smiling when he climbed out of his father's pickup. The surgeon had insisted he be examined again in Gallup. He was amazed by the new X-rays of the nearly severed arm. Bone, muscles completely healed. Full function.

He rapidly climbed the ladders up to his father's house. Found him in the kitchen, working alongside his wife.

Without turning around, Louis Paul asked, "Recognize this?"

Summer began late, the annual grasses were behind schedule. Tito looked at the tied bundles. Long, broad, rough-leaved blades. Smooth sheaths. Hairy seeds in the center.

"Wild oats. Young."

"Correct." Louis Paul had already filled a bowl with the seeds. Now poured one-hundred-per-cent Vodka over them. Stirred. The concoction grew milky, smooth. "Book on my work bench. Put recipe in your memory."

THE HANDBOOK OF PHARMACY AND THERAPEUTICS—1929.
Eli Lilly Co.
Tincture of Green Wild Oats

This medicine is used for many ailments, but is perfect for treating the depression of strong, masculine, self-assured people when their strength is burnt out. Some event happens in their lives which is of great importance, such as the death of a loved one, or breakup of a marriage. The medicine gives internal peace and calm, clear thinking, helping the patients to accept the loss, allowing their minds to plan, to organize thoughts and action.

"Where did you find this?" asked Tito.

"My Father passed it to me. Another medicine taken by white men." He poured the tincture into the *chuleya:we*. Mutton, potato, red chile, garlic, cilantro, water. Simmered for hours.

Tito dipped a finger, tasted the broth. No change of aroma or taste.

"Put in jars for doctor. We feed his soul so his mind will be cured. Otherwise, his grief will devour him."

Jack was completely still, eerily still. Not what she expected. Finally he said in a raspy voice, "Am I hallucinating or is it really you? I'm so tired..."

"Jack, come here, come to me." She held his head in her lap and leaned against the cave wall. "Sleep, Jack. Sleep. We'll talk later."

He closed his eyes, shivered involuntarily. Relaxed ever-so-slowly.

Hours later, he munched on peanut butter crackers from her pack. She sliced an apple, handed him a piece. He looked at it before he ate it.

"You haven't slept since you got here, have you?"

"No, but I'm okay. I can't explain it. Somehow I knew I was supposed to wait for you—you need to tell me something."

"News from Chicago. Do you feel good enough to answer some questions?"

"Lead me, Lori. I'm not connecting too well. Like there are dead circuits in my head. When the electricity does come back on, my brain overheats and I blow a breaker again. I can't make small talk. What do you want from me? What do I know?"

"I talked to Bill. About the radioactivity around here. You weren't at Black Rock long, did you and Bill talk much—other than patient care?"

"Yes, he told me a lot. He's obsessed, and rightfully so, with what happened here." He pulled off his T-shirt.

"You've lost weight. How much?"

"I wrestled in college, a welterweight. Had to stay about one-hundred-and-sixty pounds."

"You're no welterweight now—you're about one-forty."

"That's the least of my worries. I want revenge, Lori, and I don't know where to go first."

"Re-focus your hatred. Work with me. You said Bill was obsessed with what happened here. Talk it out, maybe something will light up."

He looked at Lori, his eyes steady. "I think I know where you're going. Bill told me about all the birth defects and lung cancer around here."

"Birth defects?"

It began with the children. Chronic lung disease. Blood dyscrasias. Leukemias. The children played on piles of fill, actual tailings from the mines. Extremely radioactive, emitting among other things, radon gas.

"And here were these kids, Bill said, playing 'King of the Mountain.'"

Simulated nuclear devices were developed at Los Alamos. Bill found out government scientists detonated nukes in what they had the nerve to call 'wasteland.' Their purpose was to track radioactive fallout patterns.

"The PhD. told him more than he should. The tests were strictly hush-hush, but strontium residues were left all over northwestern New Mexico.

Much of the contaminated property was reservation land," Jack said. "He laid out the scenario for me."

Indiscriminate tests were carried out involving Tabun—ethyl N-dimethyl phosphoroamido-cyanidate—a chemical normally stored in silver-lined glass vessels for safety. When orders came down to discontinue work on Tabun, the vessels were dropped from low-flying planes over Zuni Salt Lake. The scientists chose the drop site after learning the Russians deep-sixed their stockpiles of Tabun in the ocean, allowing the salt in the water to deactivate and destroy the deadly substance.

"I stayed at Bill's house the other night. Not with him. He told me someone eventually found an unbroken vial out there, took it home where this little kid played with it and accidentally broke it. The four-year-old died in three hours," said Lori.

"Inhalation and absorption through the skin and oral mucus membranes, " said Jack.

"Extremely toxic. Bill called it blatant genocide. He said he'd started drinking because of it."

"And the lung cancer?"

"Strange, isn't it. All this clear blue sky, clean air, star-filled nights."

"More apple?"

"Thanks. He talked about the mining east on Navajo land, near Mount Taylor."

"For uranium?"

"Right.

Lori thought back to the intel. The Mob was buying uranium ore in Canada. Transporting it across Lake Michigan—maybe to Chicago. Or Gary, Indiana. Possibly the Wisconsin coast. She decided not to press him further.

Time to get Jack to a new location. If she could find him, others could.

27

"Time to move," said Lori.

"Follow me," he said, not looking back. At the top, Lori surveyed the terrain. "Looking for something?" Jack asked.

"There it is, perfect—that small lake."

"I spotted it before, wondered if it was contaminated, but I've seen cattle and sheep grazing there. Let's go," he said.

Closer to the lake, they found a sheepherder's hut made of thick timbers with a hide hanging over the entrance. It was protectively tucked into a hollow in a rock wall, shaded by a cottonwood tree.

"We stay here," said Lori.

"You can, I'm heading back to Zuni." He was already jogging backward. "I know the way—I memorized landmarks from the air." He spun around and sprinted away.

Lori broke into a run, caught up, grabbed his arm. "No!"

He jerked free of her grip, wildness had returned to his eyes. A twitch in his right cheek.

"I've got to tell you something." She hesitated, wondering if he could handle more. "This is complicated. We know the Chicago Mob is buying uranium-rich ore from Canada. Once the ore makes it to Chicago, it's processed, concentrating it into yellowcake. We think they plan to store the cake until they can sell it. Probably a foreign country. A terrorist group.

"There's one big problem—the radioactive stuff will have to sit around for a while, it could be discovered as radioactivity builds up. They need a place where radioactivity pre-exists—like here, in New Mexico."

She looked at the ground. "Your family—had to have been killed for a reason. Your family—could they have been a part of..."

"Fuck you!" He was on the run, legs pumping, head back.

A sudden, emboldened voice thundered through the canyon. "Stop, Doctor. Stop!"

Jack spun around. Tito was standing fifty feet away. Long hair shining, looking strangely huge to him.

Dressed like a general contractor in khaki slacks, blue shirt, boots, Gabriel waited in the shadows, baseball hat low on his forehead. Bill Newman and a big black dog were jogging in the early light toward the reservoir. Disappearing into the willows and tamaracks. Half an hour later, they returned. The dog wanted more, but Newman was covered with sweat.

Gabriel waited a few minutes, before slipping across the quiet street. A small frosted window was cracked open a few inches. He heard the shower running.

A rustle caught his attention. He turned to see the big Newf wandering toward him, wagging his tail, on the other side of a chain-link fence. He reached over and ruffled the soft fur behind the dog's ears. The dog lifted up on his hind legs and licked his face. Gabriel withdrew a stiletto-like knife, plunged the knife into the dog's chest, puncturing the left ventricle.

The dog let out a soft groan, then dropped heavily to the ground.

◈ ◈ ◈

Mr. K stood on the wharf watching the Laker maneuver into its slip at Lake Calumet Harbor. The captain waved from the forward house of the ship, a bulk carrier designed for traversing the Great Lakes, also capable of negotiating river locks.

The Laker was at the larger end of lake carriers, capable of bulk loads of ore weighing ten-thousand DWT. All five holds were filled with gravel taken from a uranium mine in the Athabasca Basin. The newly discovered McArthur River Mine in the Northwest Territories was proving to be the world's largest high-grade source of uranium. Prices were soaring. The bill of lading, facilitated with Knapp's kick-backs, declared the cargo as fossil-rich shale. Clearing US Customs was a piece of cake—literally.

Dump trucks waited. Huge gantry cranes removed the cargo, dumping at a rate of one-hundred tons per hour. As each truck filled to capacity, the driver cranked a canvas cover over the cargo and departed for the processing plant. An empty truck immediately moved forward to take its place.

A huge shipment this time, enough to supply world demand. At today's rate of thirty to forty dollars a pound, worth multimillions.

Back at his office, he placed a call to Senator Trask. "Joseph, the biggest load of ore has just arrived. We've got to get this stuff out of here as soon as we process it."

"The House has passed an amended version of the Senate bill. It's coming back to us today."

"Finally—will it pass?" asked Knapp.

The senator said he had a guarantee. A colleague. Senator Richard Phillips of New Mexico.

"Father sent supplies for the two of you," said Tito. "You guys hungry?"

"How did you know Lori was here?" Jack asked. Tito shrugged. "Any messages from your father?"

Tito shook his head. "No. I'll be back tomorrow."

"I'm going back with you."

"No, you're not," snapped Lori, placing her hand on her pistol. "I'm not going to kill you. Just maim you. I mean it."

"I must leave," Tito said. "Father is waiting."

"No, hold on," said Jack. "What is anyone doing to find out who murdered my family? Why the hell are they after me? I'm damned tired of hiding like some chicken-shit rabbit, stuck in a hole."

"I understand," said Tito, glancing at Lori's drawn pistol. "It's hard for a man like you. You must trust us. We are working for you."

"He's right," said Lori

"Why are you all sounding so caring all of a sudden?" Jack glared at Lori.

"Agent Wilson, are you okay?"

"I'm fine. He's tired. I'll take care of him."

Tito disappeared into a vast shadow. Heat radiated from red sandstone cliffs to the west. A minute later, his outline re-appeared against the metamorphic rocks a mile away.

Lori sighed as she slipped her gun into her holster. "Give it up. You need to rest. There's a lot ahead of us."

Jack refused, screaming, "What the hell is going on with you? If I've got it straight, you think my family has something to do with the Mob. How could you?"

Signaling with the palm of her hand, Jack became silent. "Listen, Jack, I'm FBI. I have to ask. Did you ever hear anything that would connect your father to them?"

"No! Goddamnit! Stop asking me questions!"

"Are you being truthful with me?" pressed Lori.

"Excuse me? Who are you to talk about being truthful? By the way, when I threatened to leave with Tito, you weren't really going to shoot me, were you?"

No reply.

Trying to remain calm, he said in a level tone, "Why do you suspect my family was involved?"

She hesitated, choosing her words carefully. "It all goes back to motive—why kill an entire family? There was no evidence of robbery, the house was essentially undisturbed. What were they involved in to get them all murdered?"

"I don't know." His face was twisted with confusion and loss. "But I sure as hell know they weren't involved with the Mob, not my father, or my brother." He began to cry, which only made him angrier.

"What about Gabriel, your uncle?"

"Yeah, he had some rocky times, but he made good. Some trouble once with local politicians, the unions. You know they play tough in Chicago—the construction business is not for sissies."

"You bet I know that. Corruption there isn't just normal, it's a fine-tuned art."

"I didn't say Uncle Gabe was corrupt. He bids well, comes in on time. He's trusted."

"Trusted by whom?"

Jack slumped to the ground and leaned against one of the knap-sacks, his eyes avoiding hers.

"You need to eat, we both do." She fished around in the other bag, finding a jar of what looked like stew. She opened the Mason jar, found two spoons. They shared the meal in silence. Darkness engulfed the valley.

28

Jack stood, pulled off his shirt and shoes, took off the rest of his clothes.

"What are you doing?"

"Going to take a bath in the lake."

"Good idea," Lori said, dropping her work shirt to the ground, and peeling off her T-shirt.

The water was cold and fresh. Wordlessly, they floated side-by-side.

Against the indigo sky, stars seemed to appear from nowhere. In minutes the sky became a canopy. Dots of light, each emitting energy. Jack knew his constellations. The Big Dipper. The two stars in the cup pointing at the North Star. He outlined the Belt of Orion, the great hunter. The Pleiades, daughters of Atlas.

She wasn't watching or listening, lost in her own thoughts. Thoughts far from astronomy.

They walked out of the shallow lake together, ducked into the hut. Thick furs were spread on the earthen floor. The smell of sweet tobacco permeated the pelts.

29

At the sound of toast popping up, Bill jumped. Mr. D'Amico, or whoever he was, had rattled him. He took a sip of coffee, reached for the butter.

Flapper ambled in beside him and let out a big sigh. He got up, opened the back door, calling for Flipper. There was no response. He called again, walking along the chain link fence. At the far corner of the yard, he stopped abruptly.

"Oh, no!" He ran the last five feet to the big dog. He carefully rolled him over. Felt warm, sticky blood on his hand. There was no pulse.

"That bastard!" he screamed.

Jack awakened to the feel of cool air streaming into the shelter. He pushed back a goatskin, eased his way past Lori, and ducked. Ground fog drifted over the shallow lake, moisture beaded on the grass.

His splashing sounds woke Lori. She parted the hide. Watched him for several minutes. The sun was in front of him, glinting off his body. A great butt, she thought, and immediately felt a warmness engulf her. She reached for her T-shirt.

She found a fire pit safely away from the wind. Dry splinters of juniper, a chunk of pitch. The match sparked, the flame caught, flared.

Two goatskins by the fire, she sat down cross-legged and wrapped the hide around her bare feet. A dragonfly. Bees. The smell of mountain sage. She found a tin of pungent dried leaves. *Ha;k'yawe.*

"Good morning," Jack said. He knelt beside her. Placed a kiss behind her ear.

He was in his jeans, still slightly damp. He traced his finger down her nose. An optimistic up-tip.

She knew what he was thinking. "Bob Hope."

"No, Romanesque, like the Borgia's."

"More like the Duke of Alba," she said with a laugh. "I'm pretty sure this is tea." Using a stick to hook the handles, she teased two tin mugs close to the flames.

"Anything to eat?"

"I found some burritos. This needs to brew for a while," Lori said, spooning leaves into the cups. "It's beautiful out here. It seems like you can touch everything miles away. Even shadows have color, an intensity I'm not used to in the city." She touched his thigh. "Do you remember what happened last night?"

"What would that be?"

"Tito left, we fought, we ate, then we went swimming. No, it was too shallow—we floated."

"I remember that."

"And then..."

"Is there something worrying you?"

"Not really, I feel the best I've felt in a long, long time," Lori said with a smile. He smiled, too. Finally. She noticed.

She reached for the brass button on his jeans. He leaned toward her, gently pushing her back on the goatskin, ready to make love to this mysterious woman again. This time he committed to memory every second of their intimacy. All the while, she said only one word: 'Yes.'

Later, Jack said, "I think my butt is sunburned."

"The water is salty, let's go."

He raced her to the shallow lake, catching her in his arms, carrying her into the frigid water. She shrieked; he laughed. A very different sound.

He helped her slip on a black T-shirt. Mrs. Jahata had thoughtfully added some clothing to their supplies. How did she know?

She ran her hand through her wet hair. "Time to dump the FBI dress code." She found the knife in the backpack and handed it to him. He gave her a choppy haircut. She scraped off the remains of her red nail polish.

"I need something to keep the sweat and hair out of my eyes," said Jack.

She took the knife, sliced off the bottom three inches of her T-shirt, then tied it around his forehead. Suddenly a rattle sounded all too close to them. He held his palm up. Her hand went to her pistol lying on the goatskin.

A rattlesnake coiled under a clump of chamisa four feet away.

"No," he whispered. "Wait."

They watched the snake, head darting, when it uncoiled as fast as either of them had seen anything move. Fangs buried in a jack rabbit. Barely a struggle. Separated jaws drew the entire animal into its mouth.

Jack tapped the fetish in his pocket. "Bill was here. He wants us to know that."

Bill thought about calling the tribal police, but knew he couldn't prove Gabriel D'Amico had done anything. Besides, the bastard knew it. He cringed, fighting his fury.

He fed Flapper and her puppies, made them all comfortable in the garage. She returned to her nest amongst a pile of blankets, garden hoses, a tennis racket, a bucket of well-chewed balls. She looked exhausted, her big brown eyes watery, glistening in the dim light. It was all he could do to keep from crying. He didn't dare upset her.

"I'll check on you every hour or so. If I can't make it, Stan said to tell you he'll come by. Take it easy, everything's going to be okay," he said to the dog. He left the lights on and locked the door.

He forced himself to go to work. He and the red-haired doctor finished clinics. Began collecting inpatient charts. The head nurse knocked. "There's a man here. Wants to see you. Should I let him in?"

"Yup, and after he comes in, call the tribal police. Tell them to get here quick, but keep it quiet. Leave my door open."

Gabriel D'Amico entered the office. Bill refused to shake his hand. He tossed the stack of charts into a bin. Half-sat on his desk.

"I'm not here to take much of your time, Bill," D'Amico said, taking a step forward. "Just a few questions and I'll be on my way." Their faces were no more than a foot apart.

Bill had dug the hole a mere hour ago and buried his beautiful, innocent dog.

"Mr. D'Amico, do you like dogs?" Bill asked in a nearly inaudible voice.

"What?"

"Dogs...do you like them?" Bill asked, staring hard at the man.

"Well, yes. Dogs have masters, masters have their dogs, but they must obey us, right, Doctor?"

Bill walked around his desk and sat down.

"Where's Jack?" Gabriel looked at his gold watch. "Half the day is almost over and I don't have time to waste. Where is he?"

"I have absolutely no idea," snapped Bill, practically growling. "TDY orders are always between the head office and the officer involved."

Gabriel leaned on Bill's desk with both arms. "Be a good boy, find out where he is. I'll give you until noon." D'Amico walked to the door and turned briefly. "The puppies are cute. Your female dog is very sweet. We Italians know how to appreciate a good bitch."

30

Five AM Central Time. Mr. K checked off the last of the convoy departing from Knapp Chemical Processing Company. Handed the clipboard to Todd Murphy, his op-manager. Under the tarps, each heavy-duty vehicle carried secure barrels of yellowcake. The huge stockpile of concentrated natural uranium, 550 metric tons, was ready for smelting into purified UO^2. Not potent enough to make a dirty bomb, yet if used in a conventional explosive device to disperse radioactive material, it could cause worldwide panic. If enriched to yield weapons-grade uranium with levels above 90%, it was ideal for weapons of mass destruction.

The new Peterbilt trucks had temporary license plates. Every glove compartment contained documents authorizing interstate delivery of the cargo. All bills of lading would clear. Two drivers would alternate, one man always on.

Mr. K was agitated. Irritated. He hadn't heard a goddamned word from Gabriel, or the illustrious senator from Illinois. Fuck them. Nothing was going to get in the way. Nothing.

Mike opened the back door of the black sedan for Mr. K. The car rolled through the thousand-acre site surrounded by huge sand berms. High-intensity security lights lit the way to the guard house. A uniformed man inside saluted. A chain-link gate topped with cyclone wire clanged shut behind them.

Back in his paneled office at home, he tried to reach the senator, but was passed on to a private secretary.

"Senator Trask was expecting your call, Mr. Knapp. He's just left for the senate floor this very moment, and said to tell you the bill looks good-to-go."

"Thank Joseph for me," Knapp said, and hung up.

Too early for Scotch. He poured a glass of orange juice from a crystal pitcher on the sideboard, topped it off with Smirnoff. His nerves were like sparking electrical lines. He had more trucks moving out the next day.

Different routes. Every detail had been considered and planned. Cost of diesel fuel. Driver rotations. Sleeper times. Truck stops. Weigh stations. Each team would radio in their location every six hours to the company's central dispatch who in turn reported directly to Mr. K.

Knapp would be in place to meet the shipments at their destination.

Gabriel left the hospital, circled back behind the row of housing, parked his rental in a jumble of mesquite brush, and climbed over the chain-link fence into Jack's back yard. He knew Jack wasn't there, but maybe something would point to his whereabouts. He moved quickly from window to window. The bedroom window was open, a faded curtain fluttered in the breeze. The unmade bed was empty. Hand on his revolver, he checked each room, then headed for the garage. The door was locked. He stepped back. Kicked hard. The cheap door popped open. A dust-covered Jeep was wedged inside.

He jogged back to the car, backed out in a spray of red dirt. Newman had two hours left to give him Jack's location. The altitude was beginning to bother him; he fought to get his breath. His chest was aching.

"Christ," he said out loud. "I can't die here. In the middle of nowhere!" He drove slowly down the dirt road to the lake. Engine off. Window down. Hard to breathe. He slumped against the steering wheel, clutching his chest. Minutes passed before the pain subsided. He managed to pull himself upright, letting his head fall back, mouth open.

He didn't hear him coming.

"Are you all right?" asked the young man, his face obscured by sunglasses and a black sash tied around his forehead. His hand was on the window.

"Yes," stammered Gabriel. "Go away! Leave me alone. I was just resting."

"E'lah:kwa." The man left as quietly as he had approached.

Gabe's hand went to his shirt pocket. He popped the nitroglycerin under his tongue. It took a while to take effect. When he began to breathe normally, he wondered if the man had really stopped to help. Or did he imagine it? He reached for the crumpled newspaper he had read at breakfast. There it was—the photograph of a young Indian leaving the hospital with his father. Caption: *Tito Jahata leaves hospital against medical orders.*

Why not, he thought. Nothing in this part of the world follows any rules. There had been an accident. A passerby pulled him from his truck and rushed him to the hospital in Gallup. The man who rescued Jahata was the new attending physician at Black Rock.

Gabriel rummaged through his duffle bag, removing an Army-issue sniper scope. He surveyed the surroundings. The lake. A dam. A single-engine plane taking off. He got out, stood on the running board, looked south. Rows of houses around the stone hospital. Pick-ups pulling into the ER entrance. A man with a backpack briskly walking away. He pulled the scope into a higher magnification. The man had removed the pack and was readjusting the straps. The pack looked heavy. The Indian looked back toward the dam, crossed the highway, and purposefully started toward the base of the mountains.

Gabriel reached through the window and grabbed the newspaper. Dr. Jack D'Amico saved the kid. Maybe the kid is helping the doc. He drove to the spot where the man struck out across the chamisa and mesquite-clogged mesa. He had to take it slow. The guy knows Jack. He owes him.

He started walking after him.

The entire FAA facility smelled of cigarette smoke and stale coffee. Crackling static and occasional cryptic comments on the communication radio were the only sounds. The single employee on duty, Jeff, stepped from the map room just as the door flung open and Bill stepped inside.

"Hey, Bill, what's the hurry?"

"Someone killed my dog, Flipper. I think a man that showed up yesterday did it. Just as I was leaving the hospital, a patient told the receptionist about seeing a stranger parked at the lake. He had a long lens, looked like he was casing things out. He left his car on the main road and headed south on foot."

"A tourist? A tourist who doesn't have a photo permit?" asked Jeff.

When Bill met urgently with Louis Paul barely twenty minutes earlier, the shiwani departed with the words, 'Bad spirits talking.' For that reason alone, Bill said, "He's no tourist. I think he's a dog-killing sonofabitch." A people killer is what he wanted to say. "Is the plane fueled?"

"What are you up to?"

"I'm starting an air search."

"No! That guy is looking for you."

"He doesn't care about me, he's after Doctor D'Amico."

◈ ◈ ◈

A sensation swept over Tito, a sensation he had felt once when he was stalked by a mountain lion. Not good.

He came to a wide, deep arroyo which he usually followed to the lake. Instead of hugging the rim, he began to crawl down the eroded channel. Before dropping out of sight, he took a 180-degree look. North and west. Three-hundred yards. A man tracking him.

Not allowing dust to rise, he slid in a crouch. He hit a shale escarpment. Unstable. No footing. He pulled off his boots and continued barefoot, using his toes to cling to the shale shards.

31

With a resounding crack, the gavel sounded for quiet.

Senator Phillips steadied his grasp on the lectern. "Since May, nineteen seventy-two, over a year ago, scoping meetings and off-highway vehicle workshops were conducted to inform the public and solicit input. I can assure you, my constituents in Catron County and the Zuni tribe are cooperating with regard to ACEC use limitations regarding Zuni Salt Lake as follows." He began to read out loud:

> "Limit motor vehicle travel to designated routes. Include fluid mineral leasing. Allow withdrawal locatable minerals on 2,861 acres of federal mineral estate within the 4,839 acre Zuni Salt Lake Protection Zone. Exclude woodcutting."

Phillips turned his head away from the podium to clear his throat, then concluded.

> "The great state of New Mexico grants full authority to the BLM to manage the 4,839-acre special management area as ACECs under the alternatives in the DRMPR/DEIS. Colleagues, I thank you for your time and interest, and your positive vote for Senate Bill 236 as amended."

A page brought over the senator's canes. Once Phillips was stable, he stepped forward, slowly heading for his seat in the senate chambers.

Two rows away, Senator Joseph Trask closed his briefing book, and turned to look up at the scoreboard. Seventy yeas. Twenty nays. Ten abstains.

Senate Bill 236 passed.

Relief settled over him. Mr. K would get off his back. His thoughts were broken as two hands gripped his shoulders.

"We did it, Joe," said the senator from New Mexico. "Lunch at the Ebbitt? I'll buy."

One-thirty PM Eastern Time. The senator from Illinois walked through the revolving doors by-passing the waiting line. He passed a wait station stacked high with a pyramid of martinis. The frosted glasses were flying to thirsty politicos. The Old Ebbitt Grill was packed. Noise volume high.

Senator Richard Phillips was already well into his drink. A waiter was at the mahogany and velvet booth immediately. Trask ordered. Double vodka martini. Up, with a twist. Smirnoff.

Phillips shifted in the booth, trying to get comfortable. His canes hung from a coat rack next to their table. The martini was helping to diminish the pain. With surprising vigor in his voice, he said, "You did it, Joe. I knew you could get those bleeding hearts from the Federal Register of Historic Places to shut up. Despite all the high-minded rhetoric from the President and Secretary of the Interior about environmental justice and Indian sovereignty, the administration steamrolled this one through. You have your pile of salt now, which the very thought of makes me thirsty." He took a sip of his martini.

"Well, Richard, you have your water for that coal mining outfit, right in the heart of the sanctuary zone." Trask's comment was rank with sarcasm. "You played the game well. I might throw you a bone some other time."

A three-tiered silver tray appeared, loaded with cold seafood on ice. "Your appetizer, Senators," said the waiter.

Phillips reddened. The bastard was turning the screws on him, tighter and tighter. If only Trask had never seen those goddamned documents. "I came through, and now I'm sick of it. Makes me want to vomit."

The Illinois senator signaled for another drink. Trask wasn't the one who chose to overlook all but one bid for the latest land acquisition for Kirtland Air Force Base in Albuquerque. He also knew Phillips had packed away a hefty profit. He had to ask. "I heard about your ranch up above Taos. How did you ever manage to...?"

Trask accepted the fresh martini, waited for the waiter to step away. "Don't give me anymore of that 'my-wife-inherited-money' bullshit. Give me a little credit. I know where she came from, and it wasn't money. It was a single-wide in Raton."

Phillips set his glass down firmly, saying, "You bastard! The single most important thing my dearest late wife believed in was preserving the land. Now you and your partners are going to rape sacred land, land that has been sacred for thousands of years."

"Especially your constituents, the Zunis, as you mentioned in your testimony this morning," said Trask. "Sentimental crap. I happen to know you're going to make a pile of money on your deal, too."

"Look, we both know that coal mines need massive amounts of water. The USGS is a quagmire. I buried the Atarque Aquifer report, but one of the survey hydrologists is claiming the mining will lower the aquifer by a minimum of four feet. That could get us in a piss-pot of trouble. This is huge."

Senator Trask closed the menu and set it aside. "That's your problem. I've lost my appetite."

As Trask left, Phillips reached for a cane, slammed it down on the table, knocking over the silver tray, sweeping chunks of crab, shrimp, and lobster across the floor.

Trask walked briskly back to his office on Capitol Hill. At the doorway to his suite, an aide approached. "With all due respect, sir, I need..."

"I'm not available for the next half hour," said Trask, brushing past her.

Seated at his desk, he opened a bottom drawer and removed a telephone, one dedicated to Senate Armed Services Committee conference calls. He dialed Mr. K in Chicago. While waiting, he thought about the New Mexico senator. Christ, what was his guilt trip about? Phillips was a liar. Flat-out avaricious. He had to be with his lifestyle.

Mr. K picked up, his usual brusque self. "Knapp here."

"It's done, by Senate concurrence of the House amendments. The bill goes to President Nixon after the Secretary of the Senate certifies. It's a go, Mr. K. You can move your trucks on to the property."

A razor-sharp shale chip buried itself in the arch of Tito's foot. He cringed, his mouth opened. A silent cry.

Behind Tito by a thousand feet, Gabriel slipped and slid uncontrollably down the side of the arroyo. Scraping, grabbing, tearing, ripping. Pockets torn. Shirttail in shreds. He shielded his face, hit bottom. Sand crystals embedded in his cuts. He spit. The spotting scope was gone.

One glance back and Tito scrambled up the shale-filled origin of the arroyo. At the top, he dodged several lechuguilla bushes blocking his path. Agave plants. Sharp-pointed leaves that could rip flesh to the bone. He shifted his pack and ran toward a wall of closely-spaced piñon trees.

Gabriel pulled his pistol from the shoulder holster and bolted up the shale outlet. His heart pounded dangerously. He leveled the pistol. Fired. A plume of dust rose where the bullet buried itself in the ground inches from Tito's bare feet.

Agave plants everywhere. "Goddamnit!" He popped a nitro under his tongue. The knife-like blades sliced his legs. He screamed, growled, plunged ahead.

Tito slipped soundlessly through the trees. The thickness of the growth made it possible for a person to miss another just feet apart. He smiled, slowed down. His confidence was short-lived. A powerful hand grabbed his leg. A sudden lightning pain shot through his left foot as Gabriel's knife severed his Achilles tendon.

With amazing strength, Gabriel crawled on top of Tito. Pinned him to the ground. Knife at his throat. "I am going to cut your throat. Watch you bleed to death, and I plan on doing it slowly unless you take me to Jack. Now!"

Tito fought for breath. Gabriel's weight was crushing. The tip of the blade entered his neck under his Adam's apple. In gasps, Tito managed to say, "Okay, okay."

"Get up, you sonofabitch."

Tito tried to stand, but immediately fell. The tendon connecting calf muscle to the heel bone was severed. He couldn't push off with his toes. "I can't walk."

"Then crawl, you animal. Pick up that pack."

Bill trotted behind Jeff to the Piper Tri-Pacer. Checked ailerons, tail, wheels. Into the cockpit, high-signed good-to-go. Hand on the throttle, he started taxiing.

The intercom light went green. A soft female voice said, "Sir, the head of central dispatch is here to see you."

"Send him in, hold all calls," Knapp responded.

Murphy had reported in. All trucks were in place. Arrival at the salt lake a day away. He clicked on the intercom. "Get me two tickets to Albuquerque—first class. Have Mike bring my car around. Leave my return flight open-ended."

32

A sudden crack of thunder jolted Gabriel. He let go. Tito collapsed. Another crack, rolling, rolling thunder. Gabriel hacked off a branch; thrust the crude crutch at Tito. Piñon and cedars choked the ground between massively tall ponderosas, blocking the light. Tito lowered his head, stumbling blindly. The clouds erupted. A deluge began.

Suddenly Tito swung the crutch at Gabriel's legs. A savage grunt. Off-balance. Gabriel jerked the branch away, viciously cracking it down on Tito's shoulder.

"Try that again and I'll beat you to death."

The man could and would. Excruciating pain. Father! Help.

"I will take you to him." Bare-footed, bleeding, he led, dragging his left leg. Hopped. Drag. Hopped. Drag.

The young Indian wasn't the first person he had crippled. He had served in World War II as a foot soldier. Northern Italy. After the Americans crossed the Po River, the officers ordered their men to slice the Achilles tendons of all German prisoners. The Allies were moving so fast they couldn't take prisoners with them.

The rain intensified. Dime-size hail began to pelt them. Gabriel's shirt stuck to his skin, white hair plastered to his head. "How much further?"

"Just ahead, a lake," answered Tito, breathing hard, shivering with pain. The crutch was digging into his shoulder. Probably broken. Cracked for certain.

Looking through the grey curtain of rain, Gabriel could barely make out the outline of a shelter about a hundred feet from the lake. "There?"

Tito stared blankly at him. Gave no reply. Gabriel shoved him toward the hut. "This gun is aimed at the back of your skull. Tell them you're hurt, you need help." He dropped to one knee, both hands holding the pistol, locked on Tito.

Tito managed a few steps, called out, collapsed in the mud. Lightning flashed. A relentless zigzag. Striking, retreating back into the dark clouds faster than his words reached the shelter.

They both heard his cry. Jack pulled back the hide, stepped out into a blast of rain. "Tito?"

Tito's eyes flickered to his right. He passed out. Jack caught the warning too late.

Gabriel knelt by Tito's side. "Hey, Jacko, it's me, Uncle Gabe. You got to help him, he's hurt pretty bad."

"What happened to him? What are you doing here? Jesus Christ, Gabe, you're the last person I expected to see. How did you..."

"I had to find you. Luckily, I met up with your supplier. I have to tell you..."

"Kind of late for that, don't you think." He wrapped his arms around Tito's upper torso, hefting him up. Tito was dead weight. "Lori, help."

"Mr. D'Amico," said Lori slowly, her hand on the butt of her weapon. Gabe's pistol was trained on her.

"Special Agent Wilson. Take out your pistol. Two fingers. Now!"

Lori did as he said. Backed inside. Gabriel yanked the hide away. His pistol was still aimed at her. "Brooks told me you were naïve. Out here all alone. No backup. Said you'd follow the Handbook. Never make a move on your own." A smirk crossed his face. "Petite little bitch with your red fingernails and mini skirt. Fucked my nephew yet?"

"Bastard!" snapped Lori.

"You're an animal!" screamed Jack, stepping protectively in front of her.

Gabe was quick. He fired at Jack's leg, just missing the kneecap. The bullet ripped through his Levi's. The smell of cordite filled the cramped hut. "You're the last one left."

"Why?" Jack cried. "Why...?"

Keeping the pistol on him, he said to Jack, "Pasquale, my **half**-brother, he was always stupid. That high society restaurant, the mansion, all his self-righteousness."

Jack looked down at Tito. "You cut his Achilles tendon. That's about as inhumane as a person can get."

"You don't know the half of it. You don't know what it was like."

"Did you kill them?" Jack let out an agonizing groan. "How could you? My entire family? Why?"

"It was necessary. Pasquale got in the way one too many times."

"In the way of what?" asked Jack, practically screaming.

"Or who?" Lori snapped.

"I almost lost everything, Pasquale refused to help. Someone bailed me out—I owed him. I got the company back in the black, in spite of your daddy."

"My Father?"

"Pasquale acted like he was above bribery, like he was pure, incorruptible. He looked down on me, so did Rose, that aristocratic bitch. I had the pleasure of watching her family suffer during the war—I went to their estate and spat on the Anitoli's land."

Jack made a guttural sound. Jaw clenched. Body rigid.

It was Lori who asked, "Who bailed you out, who do you owe? How do you know Brooks?"

"Brooks, a self-serving bastard. Ass-kisser. He's just a paid lackey, on Mr. K's payroll. I had to do it. Don't you understand? Your grandfather would've done the same. Christ, he worked his butt off for everything so you, your worthless brother, those oh-so-cute sisters could have it all."

"What could be so goddamned important about one of your fucking buildings, some skyscraper or shopping mall, that you could actually kill them? And who the hell is Mr. K?"

Gabriel stared at Jack, expressionless. "Pasquale called me late after the party he gave for you. When he left the dinner table, it was to confirm a deal I had going in Canada—it wasn't shale for our cement plant, but uranium ore that I bought for Mr. K in the Athabasca Basin. Your father threatened to expose me. Uranium ore," he repeated. "Refines into yellowcake. Worth millions. You, you little prick wouldn't have to practice a day in your worthless life." He paused to wipe the sweat from his forehead.

Jack's right fist caught him squarely on the jaw. Sent him backwards. Rain, mud. He threw himself on top of Gabe. Knocked the gun away.

"Did you steal my father's watch?" Jack growled, pinning him down.

"Yes," Gabe spit. "Gave it to my bodyguard." His knee viciously caught Jack in the crotch.

He doubled over, vomiting, gagging. Gabriel jumped him from behind. Knocked him to the ground. Wrapped both hands around his neck, applying every ounce of strength he possessed.

Jack choked, gasped. Clawed the ground, legs flailing. Lori lunged at Gabriel, kicking his head. She slipped, fell beside Jack. He grabbed Lori. Ran. Stumbled. Ran. Anywhere to get away.

The rain intensified, driving like nails, pinning them down. Lightning hit the ground with a jolting repercussion. Recharged. Negative charges zigzagged from earth to sky. A giant flash cracked overhead, generating a bolt of static energy. The ball of blinding light ignited the darkened sky and detonated, sending an ionized shower to the ground. The wind, horribly confused, howled. Thrashing limbs, shredding leaves. Mud, debris combined in a sodden, swirling mass. The swirling mass metamorphed into the appearance of hundreds of slithering rattlesnakes.

Gabriel screamed. The sound was horrific. Staccato rattling gone insane. Pelting rain like fangs sinking into his flesh. He flailed, incapable of striking out.

A hideous, terrifying sound roared behind Gabriel. He spun to face an enormous grizzly bear. Dark brown hump, concave face. Fast, coming straight for him. He frantically scrambled for his pistol. Heart racing. Managed to fire. Struck the bear's right shoulder.

It reared back on two feet and roared, exposing huge canines. Giant claws, the length of a human finger, swiped Gabriel's face, ripping off his nose. Gouged out both eyes. The other paw swung, peeling off his entire face. The carotid artery gushed. Grunts. Growls. Gnashing teeth.

Gabriel's tortured scream suffocated in his own blood.

The monstrous bear lumbered away, dragging the body. Disappeared.

At his work bench, Louis Paul grabbed his right shoulder. Flinched in pain. Shut his eyes. Covered his ears. Rocked back and forth.

Standing at the door, his wife watched her tortured husband.

33

Albuquerque Sunport. Mr. K told Mike to rent a car. Half an hour later they were in a dark sedan crossing the Rio Grande. Huge old cottonwood trees bordered the slow-flowing river. Thickets of salt cedar bloomed like pink cotton candy at the edge of the brown water. Widely-spaced raindrops began to pelt the windshield. Then came a deluge.

"Where's the rain coming from?" asked Knapp from the back seat. "This is desert."

"Storms from the Sea of Cortez. A friend told me there's a monsoon season here, can you believe it?" said Mike. Minutes passed before he asked, "Fill me in, Mr. K, where're we headed?"

"Stay on Eighty-five, south to Socorro." Passing through Belen, the storm down-sized to a light drizzle. Knapp noticed a pay phone adjacent to a two-pump filling station and told Mike to stop.

He called his secretary collect. "Any word yet from D'Amico?" The secretary was silent. "I said anything from Gabriel D'Amico?"

Finally she said, "Mr. K. Gabriel D'Amico is dead."

"What?"

"Tribal police found him. He was mauled to death by a bear. They said it was pretty bad, nothing left of his face. State police traced him back to a rental car he got in Albuquerque."

Knapp hung up, opened the glass door. Mike held an umbrella. "Jesus, killed by a bear," he said in a hardly audible voice.

The driver slid behind the wheel, looked at the rearview mirror, asking, "What was that, sir?"

"A bear killed Gabe D'Amico, a goddamned bear. Just like Mario. Shit!"

The storm clouds lowered, rainfall increased. The highway twisted and dipped through arroyos. Yellow danger signs warned of flooding. Pungent grey-green chamisa hugged the road.

"When we get to Socorro, look out for Manzares Avenue, take a left," Knapp said. "Down the block, there's a hotel on the left. The Valverde. Check us in; I'll be in the bar."

Locals packed the smoke-filled bar, a jukebox resounded with Credence Clearwater. The crowd was a mix of hippies from New Mexico Tech and bikers. Seated in a booth against the far wall, Knapp ordered a double Scotch. He had trouble seeing the waitress's face; the flashing red and green lights of the jukebox made the corner seem even darker.

Mike, despite being six-foot-four and upwards of two-fifty, slid smoothly into the booth. He still wore his raincoat, a coat that hid a pistol-grip shotgun. "Bags are in the rooms. Pretty crappy, but the bathrooms are okay."

"What did you expect?" said Knapp, draining his glass. His right hand clutched a wet cocktail napkin, which he waded into a tiny ball. "Both men killed by bears. Maybe once, but twice? What are the odds?"

"I'll be at your side every minute. Don't worry, Mr. K."

"Easy for you to say. We leave at dawn. The advance team should already have started digging."

Restless, Louis Paul rose early, grabbed a couple of corn tortillas and left the still-dark pueblo. He was accustomed to navigating the pueblo in the dark. Electricity wasn't introduced to the area until the late 1950's; the first domestic water system didn't come to the pueblo until the sixties. Before that the people siphoned water from springs, hauled it back to the pueblo in barrels. Mules pulled the wagons. He chopped wood in the freezing cold as a kid. Snow, blinding, stinging winds. Animals froze to death. Nothing to eat. The people starved.

He crawled into his pickup and drove south-by-east, toward a rare, high desert lake, a site considered sacred to Zunis and other Pueblo Indians. The Acoma, Laguna, Hopi and Taos, as well as Apaches and Navajos all revere the *Ma'l Oyattsik'i*, the Salt Mother deity. Pilgrimages were vital. Trails radiated in all directions.

Only four-feet deep at most, the dry season evaporation reduced the lake to a small pond near the center, a geologic crater, or maar, leaving exposed salt beds, some of the earth's finest. Native Americans annually collected it—both for eating and ceremonial purposes.

To Louis Paul the lake was the umbilical cord tying all Indians together. Even in times of inter-tribal wars, they camped side-by-side in the presence of the Salt Mother in sort of a Neutrality Zone. All tribes were not allowed to even kill game or attack an enemy. All creatures were free to come and go without molestation. For him, as a Zuni, this place was the center of the world. Center of his son's world, and Tito's sons to be.

The Feds seized the lake in the 1880s, treating the 18,000 acres as wasteland. The thought burned in the back of his throat. He was no idealist. He did not believe in the American dream. Real power exists in nature, like a rainstorm, a river. Real time is Indian time.

A shadow flashed on the windshield. A red-tailed hawk circled, riding the air currents. He took his eyes off the road and spoke to the majestic bird. "We were here before them. We will be here forever."

The lake, bordered by forest and high mesas to the north, sat in a valley reaching west like a broad fjord opening to the sea. He made a sharp left hand turn onto a barely decipherable track. The truck bucked. Steep rises, sudden drops. He hit a sandy arroyo, choked with chamisa and tightly bordered by Russian olive trees. Thorny branches struck the cab, sending screeching noises into the air. Suddenly the two front wheels were in the air, hanging over a precipitous drop-off. Back tires spun the sand for control. He already had the truck in low gear. Shifted in reverse. Back to low. Back to reverse. He could smell burning rubber as the clutch screamed, the motor roared. The truck swerved, grabbed, pitched hard to the right. Steering into the slide, the truck bed swung back and forth until he was finally able to straighten out, scooting backward to solid ground.

The engine sputtered, stopped altogether, rolling to a stop in a maze of creosote brush. After repeated attempts to start the engine, he gave up, slid from the truck and began climbing to the top of the purple mesa. The sanctuary below was surrounded by a few grass clumps and tenacious, bent trees.

He spotted clouds of dust in the distance. Wind devils, he thought at first. Squinting in the brilliant rising sun, he watched the dust plumes grow closer. He knelt, focusing on a line of trucks that were moving toward the south edge of the salt flats where a yellow backhoe was digging, belching exhaust.

"Coal miners," he muttered in disgust, knowing they would anger the Salt Mother. The region couldn't afford to lose more water. "When the water is gone, it's gone, and She will leave," he worried aloud. His grandchildren's future could be lost, drained for the white man's profit. He slid down the hillside. Broke into a hard run.

Back in the stalled truck, he pumped the gas pedal. Tried the starter. Grinding. Silence. He climbed out, opened the hood. His eye caught something in the sand, a cigarette butt, then another. Tracks, but definitely not Indian tracks. The footprints, like the butts, were recent.

He read the sign—the left print dragged. A limp. The right showed weight on the heel. About one-hundred-sixty pounds.

The Piper climbed easterly toward El Morro. A reliable waterhole was hidden at the base of the giant sandstone bluff. He knew the Headland Trail well, uneven and worn. Always leaving him blistered and sunburned after the climb.

Searching for signs of Jack, Bill began a slow turn south, setting a new course due west, paralleling the route he had just flown. For an hour-and-a-half, he flew a crisscross, low-level search pattern, gradually working further south over Fence Lake, between Circle Butte and Santa Rita Mesa.

Zuni Salt Lake came into view.

Seeing a lingering trail of dust in the otherwise crystal-clear sky, he broke his pattern to check it out. Trucks were moving across the salt flats toward a waiting Caterpillar. Not just any heavy-duty trucks. Sidelifters. Specialized to hoist and transport intermodal containers. Capable of loading/unloading giant containers using hydraulic-powered cranes mounted at each end of the chassis.

He climbed in altitude. Made a wide loop, directly over a dark sedan which turned off State Road 601 in the direction of the trucks. Refuel. Get to Louis Paul.

34

"Hold him tight, Lori," Jack said, positioning her hands on Tito's shoulders.

"Shouldn't we get him to the hospital?"

"No. The tendon is retracting and the longer we wait..."

They had dumped all the supplies from the knapsacks and Lori's bag. A sewing kit from the hotel. Jack—duct tape and a coil of 6# test monofilament fishing line. Selecting his 'instruments,' he carefully flashed them with a match to sterilize them.

Without anesthetic, Jack used pliers to pull the tendon attached to the heel bone at the back of the ankle. A lateral slice. He removed a one-inch piece of tendon, producing a notch.

Tito uttered not a sound.

Identical procedure to the tendon attached to the calf muscle. Piecing two tendon sections together, overlapping them at the site of the notches. He broke out the fishing line, threaded it, and began sewing the tendons together. Attachment completed. Skin pulled into place, taped. Only then did he look at Tito's face. It was twisted, pale. Sweat beaded above the upper lip and brow.

"You did great, Tito," Jack said softly. "You did great." A strip from his own T-shirt covered the surgical site.

Lori kissed Tito on the forehead, brushed back his damp, black hair, and said, "I'll be right back."

"Sick?"

"No, I'm okay." The rain had stopped; clear sky appeared above low clouds. Blood-stained earth stood out starkly where Gabriel's face had been gutted. Standing beside the dark sienna stain, she tried to sort out Gabe's last statements. Brooks, her own boss, was deeply involved. Was Josh Flores working for Brooks or did Yolanda send him as her contact?

The name—Mr. K? Lori knew Chicago's high-rollers, good and bad. Closing her eyes, she used her alphabetized memory to pull a file from a cabinet in her brain. (A talent separating her from most of the men at Quantico.)

Mr. K.

Knapp. Society column. She pictured a man in a tuxedo, hair combed back. Caption: *Mr. K Saves Ravinia Festival Season.* Major philanthropist on the Chicago scene. D. C., too. Lots of people were on Knapp's payroll. Could he be the puppeteer? Did he order the D'Amico murders?

If she was right, she had to prevent both Brooks and Knapp from knowing Jack was still alive.

Bill decreased the plane's altitude to better see. Headed north to the airport. A deserted truck caught his eye. He dipped, recognized the brown pickup. He nosed the plane closer to the ground, banking to make a second pass. Louis Paul stepped back from the hood, waving as he watched the plane descend.

Bill pulled up, but too late. He crashed in a tangle of tall sagebrush. Sinewy branches grabbed at the undercarriage. The wheel collapsed, swinging the Piper around. A full 180-degree spin. An abrupt stop. Threw him against the door which flung open. The left wing was crushed.

Louis Paul ran through the coarse silver-grey growth to the crippled plane. "Doctor Bill!"

"I'm okay. Goddamn! Where did that tree come from?" He slid to the ground. A strong pungent odor emanated from gouged brush. "Whoa, we're outa luck—shit on a stick." A nasty gash over his left eye. Bruises on both wrists.

"Steady, Doctor Bill. Sit."

"No time." He lurched back to reach under the pilot seat to grab his pistol. "Where's Jack?"

"Not far, FBI woman, Tito, too."

"Got to get them out."

Jogging ahead, Louis Paul grabbed a pack from his truck bed. Headed south. Ten minute run to a solid wall of sandstone. He pointed to a barely visible crevice, flashed a rare smile. "How many burritos today, Doctor Bill?" He raised the pack above his hat, got a foothold with the toes of his boots and pulled himself into the slit, face pressed sideways against the stone.

Bill stuck his gun in the back of his waist and followed, sidestepping along the foot-wide channel. Narrow, and climbing vertically. Within twenty feet, the crevice widened. Crowned out above a shale-laden drop-off.

Louis Paul crouched on the edge of the precipice. Bill dropped to his knees beside him. "God, I could use a beer."

"I put plug in the jug a long time ago. Water?" Louis Paul handed him a battered canteen.

Bill took a long drink, coughed. "You saw the trucks?"

"Yes."

"Where's Jack?"

Louis Paul pointed down the shale slope and jumped.

Lori was the first to see them, and yelled to Jack, "It's Louis Paul. Bill's with him."

"Hey, man," he said, with a pounding hug to Jack. "Been looking for you. A guy dropped by, said he was your uncle." Bill stopped to catch his breath. "The bastard killed Flipper, threatened me. He's looking for you."

"Gabriel." Jack pointed to the blood-stained ground. "He's dead." He put a hand on Louis Paul's shoulder. "He hobbled your son."

Louis Paul dropped to his knees beside Tito. Held his hand above the bandaged ankle.

Tito winced. He touched Lori on her forearm, gave a shrug toward the outside. She left with him. Neither said a word.

The compliment to Lori was unspoken. Louis Paul wanted her company. He ducked into a grove of tall ponderosa.

"You observe," Louis Paul said finally. "Respond." He held a dense pine branch back for her to pass.

"Yes," said Lori.

"We are in an endless Sea of Spirits. Things appear in different physical forms. You know this, don't you?"

She nodded. Stopped walking. "I don't grasp the organized idea of a force. I don't get it. But I do believe there is a spiritual world practically without boundaries."

"You are right. You are wise. Like my fetish." He showed his prized carving, a small bear. "I revere it. It is my mediator between human and spirit worlds. Man is most vulnerable. The fetish, if treated right and true, has a living power. When this is over, we talk more."

They emerged on the edge of a vast grassy meadow. He ducked down, made a few quick slices with his knife. Tucked the cuttings under his arm. "We go back now."

Returning with a clutch of sagebrush, Louis Paul was already pulverizing stripped leaves.

"No time for a poultice," he murmured. "It's okay, doctors, I promise." He removed the bandage. His hands worked fast, with great strength. Crushing silver-grey leaves and sap. A paste applied on the incision. Covered with a piece of his shirttail. Bound with bark strips. "Topical dressing. Halts internal bleeding, infection."

"I was worried about that," Jack said.

"Doctor Bill, tell what you saw at Salt Lake."

Trucks. Sideloaders. Caterpillars digging. Lots of motion. A trailer. Then he remembered the black sedan. "I could just make out their silhouettes—a big guy was driving, another guy was in the backseat. I climbed and got the hell out of there."

"A man in the backseat with a chauffeur?" asked Lori.

"You think it was the guy on my tail?" said Jack.

"Yes, and I think I know who he is."

Director Clarence Kelley, at one end of the conference table surrounded by FBI brass, was fuming over a confidential report from Chicago regarding the Gary, Indiana Port of Entry. He pushed a stack of yellowed and smudged bills of lading down the table. Someone in the agency, his agency, was helping to facilitate illegal shipments. And Kelley certainly didn't think it was being pulled off by some petty thief in Canada.

The Deputy Director reminded him that Canada had some of the richest ore in the world. Radioactive uranium. Lots of money.

Kelley demanded to know more. Details were presented regarding uranium mining in New Mexico, particularly on the Indian reservations. Plus the added fact that a recently passed Congressional Bill relocated a boundary in far western New Mexico, placing Zuni Salt Lake under the jurisdiction of the Bureau of Land Management. A site sacred to the natives.

Kelley, clearly agitated, wanted to know the lake's connection with radioactive uranium.

"Salt is an excellent material for controlling the natural radium released by purified uranium," said the FBI's top Cointelpro agent.

"Who sponsored the legislation to get that boundary relocated?" asked Director Kelley.

Like his crew, Knapp dressed in khaki slacks, tan shirt, desert boots.

Black baseball cap, big dark glasses. Standing beside his ops manager, he looked like everyone else. 104°. Knapp's shirt was sweat-ringed. He took off his glasses, wiped the lenses, squinting in the wavy light.

Yellow Caterpillar backhoe loaders systematically removed salt in a staked grid layout. Like an archaeological dig site. Knapp's design, his plan. The cross-country transfer, everything from a catering truck to portable toilets. If the men were comfortable, they didn't mind twelve-hour shifts, night and day.

The only thing Knapp didn't provide was a Geiger counter.

Diesel exhaust fumes belched. An oily heat haze wavered over the dry lake like a suspended mirage. Shift change. Men emerged from air-conditioned sleeping compartments in the trucks to swap places.

Knapp checked his blueprints. Half of the containers had been off-loaded from the sidelifters, buried, and covered with salt. Empty trucks enroute to Chicago. He slapped the op-manager on the back. "Murphy, schedule on target. I'm proud of you. I'll be back at the beginning of the night shift."

His driver had the air conditioning on high, the back door open. As Knapp slid into the backseat, Mike handed him a leather pouch, saying, "I was talking to the caterer. Interesting fellow, married a Zuni woman. When she found out he was delivering stuff out here, she insisted he get her some salt. Said it has healing powers. The guy was also getting some for his mother, rheumatoid arthritis, can't use her hands. I got some for you; maybe help your tennis elbow."

Knapp loosened the strings, tasted the blue-tinted salt. "Indian bullshit. But I'll keep it—a token of the op."

35

It was early evening when Senator Richard Phillips landed in Santa Fe aboard a constituent's twin-engine Beechcraft King Air 90. His black Cadillac sedan was spotted with rain. The fragrance of damp chamisa filled the mesa surrounding the small airport. He hefted his briefcase into the back seat. Sat heavily behind the wheel. One by one, he pulled his legs into the car. Two canes hit the passenger seat. He had business to take care of in the state capitol before heading to Taos, and he needed a drink.

Canyon Road. Left on a rutted driveway, gated condos, a dark gallery. Parking opposite the entrance to The Compound.

The maître'd was prompt. "Senator, your table is ready. Or perhaps a cocktail in the bar first?"

"I'm meeting someone. The bar. A vodka martini, Victor, you know how I like it."

Twelve bleached-oak stools on three sides of a low pit serving station. A frosted glass appeared. Shaved ice, chilled vodka. Sheeting on the glass, a scent of lemon.

Ready for a second, his guest walked in. "Make that two martinis," Phillips said.

Victor led them to the rear dining room to a banquette beneath a large brass sun sculpture. He stood to the side as the senator slowly made his way to the table. The long flight from Washington had taken its toll. The maître'd held out his arm to steady him and palmed the twenty-dollar tip without saying a word.

"I like this place, spare, clean design. Girard is a genius."

"Richard, we've got to talk."

Phillips didn't like his tone. "It's Senator. First names later. You and your board have your lease. Eighteen-thousand acres waiting to be strip-mined. Enough coal to last fifty years."

"But...we've got problems. A hydrologist from the BIA has filed a complaint with the goddamn Equal Employment Opportunity office. Says your office harassed him after he found hydrological studies verifying our mine would damage Zuni Salt Lake."

"No one from my office would be stupid enough to do that. Go after him. You can afford the best lawyer," said Phillips. "I'll get you the gold list."

"We're facing contempt of court. Goddamnit. Phillips, I thought you buried those BLM files." The coal executive's face reddened. "Senator, to process the coal, we've got to use six-hundred gallons of water per minute—all from that aquifer."

"I know that! You've got the water rights—I came through. What are you so goddamned worried about?"

"You know what's happening out there? Right now! Bunch of big rigs are messing around at the Salt Lake. Huge containers. They're burying them in the salt beds."

"So what? Doesn't have anything to do with you. Or me."

"My people investigated. Those containers are radioactive. The water in the aquifer will be contaminated. Drink the water anywhere on that reservation and you'll glow in the dark. No good for our use. The deal's off. And, forget any more contributions."

A stunned Senator Phillips sat alone.

"Trask," he said aloud when he finally reached his car.

Director Kelley had read the report from the Chicago Port Authority and he was not a happy man.

First, random sampling of cargo against bill of lading showed marked discrepancies. The cargo was reported to be shale gravel, but in fact, it was high quality uranium ore.

Secondly, several shipments, over three weeks in same time period, had come up with the same results.

In conclusion, the findings had been forwarded to the Chicago office of the FBI.

He hit the intercom button and told his secretary to get someone from Cointelpro. An expert on uranium toxicity.

Clarence M. Kelley was new to the FBI as top boss, but had actually entered the FBI as a special agent in the fall of 1940. The year he took over was chaotic. A bungled burglary occurred in June of 1972. Less than five weeks after Hoover died in his sleep. Next two acting directors didn't survive the 'politically sensitive' climate on the Hill, so the Bureau chose an insider to take on the challenge.

A thirty-ish kid in a black suit stood in front of the director fifteen minutes later, reading from a notepad. In a flat voice typical of the special agents chosen for the agency's high-threat team, he told Kelley that the Senate Committee on Government Ops had oversight of the AEC.

"Over the Atomic Energy Commission?" Kelley said rhetorically. "Well, I'll be damned. Who heads that up?"

The agent responded immediately. "Senator Joseph Trask, sir."

"Well, well." A smile crossed the director's face. "I didn't come out of retirement for this kind of crap. First Watergate, now this. I'm going to make a friendly call to the illustrious senator from Illinois."

36

Tito moved his foot. Grinned.

"Be careful," said Jack. "You're going to pull something loose."

"No. Must start moving ankle," said Louis Paul in a soft monotone. "Almost dark. Let's go."

Bill touched Jack's arm. "Take these," he said, handing up a pair of binoculars. "We'll catch up, Tito knows the long way."

Louis Paul bounded up the shale deposit, threw a rope back to Lori. Reeled her up, then Jack. No talk. Flat on the ground out of sight, they studied the activity below.

Men worked as a unit. What trucks weren't excavating or hydraulically unloading were idling, cooling the cabs.

Shift change. Rested drivers on the night shift exchanged places. A small white van arrived, delivering boxes of what appeared to be dinner and cold drinks to the now off-duty crews. Two boxes were also deposited at a trailer.

Jack passed the binoculars to Lori, whispering, "See the two guys by the car. Recognize either?"

"Maybe, the shorter man. The one walking away toward that trailer. It's pretty dark, but I think I know who he is. If it fits in with what I've been thinking, his name is Anthony Knapp."

"Mr. K?" said Jack. Vaguely familiar. Then he remembered. Intermission at the Lyric Opera. In the men's room. Jack was the on-call house physician. When he took his aisle seat, he watched the guy glad-hand his way to a fifty-yard-line seat. Seemed everyone knew his name. What the hell was Anthony Knapp doing in New Mexico?

Bill and a pale Tito appeared beside them.

"This is very bad," said Louis Paul. "We got to stop them. They are desecrating our land."

'We only have two weapons," whispered Lori.

"Give me one of them," said Jack.

"No," said Lori. "You're the magnet. We stand a better chance of getting him if you stay out of it."

"She's right. There are other ways," interjected Louis Paul, nodding to his son.

"That bastard down there may have ordered the killing of my entire family. The pieces are coming together. You're not going to keep me from..."

"Keeping you alive is my job," said Lori.

"Listen to her," repeated Louis Paul.

Jack dropped his head on folded arms, his nose inches from the red soil.

Louis Paul motioned to Lori and Bill. Bending one finger and gesturing toward Jack, he signaled his son. Tito pressed both hands on the base of Jack's spine.

Jack could not move.

Louis Paul silently worked down the hill toward the sacred flats, using sparse clumps of chamisa as cover. He pointed to Bill, then to the man who had just gone into the trailer, signaling an arc.

To Lori, the backhoe. She moved quickly to a newly created pile of salt near the Caterpillar. Louis Paul slithered onto the open flat salt bed, watching Lori, his eye also on Bill. Both moved into place.

She was first to make a move. In a crouched position she slipped toward the belching Caterpillar, coming up behind the cab. Just as she started to grab the side rail and climb up, the 4 x 4 loader backhoe coughed. Shut down. The operator stepped out of the lighted cab. She crouched down, but the driver spotted her. He took two huge steps forward, before flying toward her. She fired.

The bullet grazed his neck but he kept coming. She attacked, sending a pant-busting crush to his crotch, and bashed her gun against his face, breaking his nose. The driver screamed, both hands clenched her windpipe. She fired a lethal round into his heart. His dead weight knocked her to the ground, a leather-gloved hand smothered her face. The smell of his sweat, oil and grease was overwhelming. She struggled to push him away but his work boots trapped her legs. Breathing heavily, using all her strength, she edged the bulk of his two-hundred-fifty pounds off. She rolled away.

Louis Paul saw everything. He rose to his feet as another engine rumbled to life. Over the bucket, the driver had him in a clear line of sight and nimbly turned the twenty-thousand-pound machine toward him. Standing in the headlights, Louis Paul watched the driver shift, increasing torque to twenty-five miles per hour, leaving huge, welted tracks on the lake bed. The driver activated the joy stick manipulating the extendable bucket, repeatedly snapping and shutting the serrated-fork edges.

A gang of off-duty workmen jumped from their semi-trucks and ran in her direction. Lori stood, legs apart, both hands on her pistol, firing precisely at each man. Five went down, their bodies a tangle. Her remaining shots pinged off yellow steel.

From his vantage point, Jack saw the backhoe thundering toward the outline of Louis Paul. He ground his teeth, clawing his nails into the clay soil. He growled, tried to bolt, but Tito's pressure on his spine paralyzed his entire body. Frozen in place.

Louis Paul stood as tall as if he were a ponderosa guarding the entrance to Zuni, silver-streaked hair flowing. The monstrous machine was so close he could see the driver's face, his day-old beard, the lowered black cap. The trenching bucket opened. A shrill screeching noise blasted forth. Bucket locked.

An ear-popping crack of lightning filled the air, overshadowing the roar of the diesel engine. The sound was huge. The salt bed gave way, a massive crevasse opened, swallowing the backhoe. The driver swiveled in his seat. Screamed. He disappeared into the rapidly flooding pit. Water frothed, waves rose. In moments, a shelf of salt developed, closing the lake's gaping wound. No sign of the giant piece of machinery.

At the trailer window, Knapp saw the brilliant flash of light. Transfixed, he listened as the sounds of the growling, groaning engine were gradually smothered. The machine was sucked into the earth.

Bill took aim at the figure in the trailer, fired. The window blew to pieces, embedding shards in Knapp's left shoulder and neck. Body hunched, gun down, Knapp dove for the door. Rolled out and under the railing, hunched under the steps. Pain registered. He pulled a leather glove on to his right hand, clenched his teeth. Pulled two jagged slivers of glass from his shoulder. A long, deadly piece in his neck. Missed the principal vessels, but bleeding was severe.

Mike fired at Bill. A miss. He dove into the back seat, scrambled to the wheel. Ignition.

Knapp fired from a crouched position. Bill sensed the blast wave preceding the hammer-like crush. Shredding a path through a kaleidoscope of nerves. Instantly, paralyzing cramps dropped him to his knees.

A second hammer punch struck Bill's right cheek, crushing his jawbone, ripping through the lower portion of his tongue, tearing the lingual artery. Blood swamped his mouth.

Louis Paul turned away from the carnage to focus on the ridge above the salt bed. Tito lifted his hands. Jack was released. They sprung in unison, ran the perimeter of the mesa, leapt over the edge. They both flew. They both knew they were flying.

Numbness crept over Bill's body. He was helpless, but managed to kick the pistol at his feet. Jack reached him, scooping up the gun just as piercing cracks punctuated the air. Lori fired at two drivers, both went down. Another returned a shot at her before swinging his semi-truck in a wide arc heading for the exit. The remainder of the sidelifters followed, red taillights disappeared into darkness.

Legs pumping, pistol leveled, Lori ran back toward the car, judging caliber and distance.

"Lori! Get down!" yelled Jack.

The bodyguard reached under the seat, pulled out a pistol-grip shotgun, and managed to get off a shot at Jack. Shot peppered the ground, sending white dust devils into the air. Jack dodged right/left/right, then somersaulted to the corner of the trailer. Simultaneously, Knapp ducked and ran, diving into the back seat of his car.

Jack stood, spread his legs, fired.

The entire back window shattered as the bullet continued, blowing off Mike's right ear. He screamed. Blood spurted. His hand on the gearshift slipped, shifting into neutral. Lori leapt for the passenger door. Tires spun. Smoked. Knapp was on the floor, hands covering his head. Ignoring the pain, Mike slammed the shift with his bloody hand, knocking it into low. The car jerked forward. He floorboarded the pedal. The side view mirror caught Lori's chin, knocking her to the ground. Stunned. The rear tire missed her head by inches.

Jack saw her go down. The car swerved, tipped to the side. He fired again through the back window. The sedan gathered speed. He emptied the weapon, but the car disappeared.

Lori brushed salt off her clothes, wincing as it ground into the gashes on her chin and elbows. She caught Jack's look of concern, but shook her head, saying hoarsely, "I'm okay. Bill...?"

37

"*B*rooks, Trask here. I suppressed the Port Authority report sent to my committee, but...someone sent it to Kelley. Who? We could be in big trouble. Find out. Take care of it. Understand?" He hung up and opened the door to the phone booth. It was ninety-five degrees and ninety-percent humidity in Washington, DC, but his hands were cold.

Brooks stared at the receiver, then cradled his head on the desk. Who the hell sent that info to Director Kelley? His hands were shaking as he began pacing.

His thoughts snowballed: Knapp was at the Salt Lake with no way to be reached. He had reported the trucks were almost finished unloading. As for Agent Wilson—the bitch was on D'Amico's trail like a coonhound. But what if the good doctor didn't know anything about his father's threat to expose Knapp and his partner? Was it Gabriel, after all?

Hell, it didn't matter what the kid knew, thought Brooks. He has to be killed. Who sent the intel to DC? Could they trace it back to his own office?

There were thirty employees working on his floor. Thirty fucking people. He slammed his hand on the conference table so hard that one of the Chinese vases fell over. He hit the intercom button. "Hold all calls and get in here, now! And bring me some ice."

When his personal secretary opened the door, she saw the vase and quickly picked up the pieces.

"We have a fucking catastrophe going on, and you're the only one I trust."

"I understand, sir. How can I help you?" Yolanda replied coolly.

Jack felt for a pulse. "He's alive." Louis Paul and Tito tore a sleeper seat out of a semi and tied Bill to the make-shift litter. Bill slipped in and out of consciousness. They ransacked the trailer. Band-Aids. A partially used roll of gauze. Methylate. Obviously the boss didn't give a shit about the men working for him, thought Jack.

"Let's turn him over on his stomach. Easy, easy. Tito, keep the pressure on his cheek." Jack handed him a fresh gauze pack. "Get me something sharp, something…"

Louis Paul palmed him a razor-sharp blade. He began to explore the wound site, but stopped.

"Got to get him to the hospital. There could be a lot more damage than I can see."

While they hovered over Bill, Tito scanned the horizon, his attention on a dust cloud, barely visible in the pre-dawn light. Pointing at the faint trail, he murmured, "A visitor, moving fast."

Brooks crunched on ice, staring at the stack of reports on his desk. Crunch.

Barely able to stand the noise, Yolanda shivered. "Want me to process those, sir?"

Her voice jolted him out of his trance. "Not yet." He motioned her away without looking up, and held up his hand, saying, "Stay. Sit."

Yolanda felt like a dog obeying her master, but she stayed put, wishing she was a male canine and could piss on him and the goddamn intel he was so upset about.

Brooks pulled the reports closer, adjusted his reading glasses and slowly read each page. A single entry caught his eye. He re-read the cryptic notation. He could hear his heart speeding up.

Mr. K to Salt Lake. Trucks arrived in NM w/o problems.

He picked up the second page. Words jumped out: *K overseeing storage. All okay.*

Brooks noticed the door was ajar. He slammed the door shut, and moved behind Yolanda's chair. Hands on the back of the chair, close to her ear, he said, "This intel. How many people have seen it?" He snatched a file and shoved it in her lap.

After glancing at the report, Yolanda said, "I don't know. Office Channels." She paused, waiting for his response. All she got was the smell of his breath. The ice hadn't helped.

"Since when? Why did Channels pick up on this?"

"Since Agent Wilson went on assignment."

"Clarify."

"She flew to Albuquerque. Went undercover. Your direct orders. The intel you are referring to have similar tags, so Channels forwarded them to you."

"Tags?"

"Well, the first tag Channels picked up was *NM*, which is obviously *New Mexico*. Then there's the capital *K* in both transmissions. Nothing serious, I hope, sir."

Brooks rounded his desk and sat down wearily. Pressing his fingers together, he looked over his hands at her for a full minute. Finally he said, "And your routine in processing these reports?"

"You mean, what do I do with them?" She steeled herself for his next blast.

"Goddamnit, yes! What happens to these fucking pieces of paper?"

"Exactly as you instructed. First to your desk, afterwards I file them according to origin and date in the classified file room."

"That's it? There are no other copies?"

"No, sir. Absolutely not."

He threw his reading glasses on the desk. "That will be all, Yolanda." As she walked to the door, he added, "Thank you."

She could still smell his sour-minty breath when she returned to her desk. Checked the time. Two hours until she could leave for lunch, place an untraceable phone call to Lori.

Despite the blood streaming into his right eye, Mike managed to head the sedan east toward Magdalena. Knapp ripped open his workshirt and tee shirt. Folded and compacted the cloth. Reaching forward from the back seat, he gently wedged the soft cloth under Mike's hand and skull. The white jersey knit quickly oozed fresh blood. "Apply lots of pressure." Knapp said. "You're going to be okay." He pulled on his shirt and slid back in the seat.

In the distance, lightning crazed across the mountains north of the tiny community. Mike glanced at the dashboard; the fuel needle wavered on empty. Panic took control.

Reduce Speed Ahead.

He slowed down; the first fat drops of rain hit the windshield, then a downpour. Lightning crisscrossed the sky. He fumbled with the wiper switch; the blades scraped the windshield, fighting the deluge. He spotted a dingy shanty with two pumps out front. No awning, no brand name. Dim light inside but no one around.

"Wait," said Knapp. "It's going to let up."

It didn't.

"I'll go get someone," said Knapp.

"Shit!" Mike snapped. "No. I'll go." He stepped into a blast of rain.

At least the water was washing off some of the blood. He reached for the pump handle with his left hand. Dropped it. He switched hands, using his left to press the cloth over the hole in the side of his head. His right hand squeezed the pump handle. Gas poured on to the sodden ground, splattering his legs and shoes.

The damn gas wouldn't flow unless he stood there and squeezed the trigger, but at least there was gas. He kept his eyes on the sky, ducking with each arcing flash. The hair on the back of his hands stood up. Static energy everywhere. Suddenly he saw nothing, heard nothing, and did not feel his body hitting the ground. A direct lightning bolt struck the car and passed through his body, grounding in the mud where he stood.

Instantly, a fireball engulfed the car and Mike's body. The full gas tank exploded.

Louis Paul took a step backward and shielded his eyes.

"What's wrong?" asked Jack.

"The man who got away...in the car...he is dead."

"You expect me to believe that?"

"I felt it. These people are desecrating Great Salt Lake Mother. She is very angry." Slowly, he knelt and looked up at Jack. "I am so tired. So tired."

Lori touched his shoulder. Louis Paul's eyes shifted to her. He placed his other hand on top of hers.

Senator Trask entered the FBI building at 601 Fourth Street in downtown DC. Summoned by the Director himself, and ushered by two special agents to Kelley's door, the senator was royally pissed by the time he was told to sit.

Kelley didn't waste time.

With no pleasantries advanced, he asked, "What are you involved in, Senator?"

Trask began to answer but stopped. He focused on the Director's desktop, spread with an array of reports, each stamped: *Zuni/Gallup.* He felt a sudden chill. Completely blindsided. He could barely talk.

Multiple questions followed rapidly. Trask responded with nothing of substance. Instead he responded rhetorically. "Why is the FBI interested? Why does this concern me?"

Kelley began a rampage. Tampered bills of lading. Illegal transports from Canada. Murderous slaughter in Chicago.

The interview ended bluntly. "Senator Trask, you can expect an in-depth investigation. A special senate enquiry."

A battered Jeep Wagoneer headed directly at them. The driver stopped thirty feet away, held up his arms, climbed out of the dusty green vehicle and limped toward them. "Doctor D'Amico?"

"Flores!" exclaimed Lori. "It's okay. I know him."

Jack glanced at Tito, Louis Paul. Both men understood: *Watch him.* Turning back to the stranger, he said, "I need to get Doctor Newman to the hospital in Gallup."

"What's wrong with him?"

"You saw," said Louis Paul.

"I'll take him. Put him in the back seat."

"Go with this man," Louis Paul said to Jack and Lori. "Watch over Doctor Bill."

With Flores at the wheel, Lori got in beside him, her service revolver in her lap. A loud crackling sound emitted from the floor beside her legs.

"It's a Geiger counter, got it in Albuquerque at the Army-Navy store," said Josh. "Beta gamma probe. Very sensitive. Only about seven pounds, works off D-batteries. Watch the dial, if it goes wild..."

"Let's get the hell outa here," snapped Jack, as he cradled Bill's head. "That's radiation-death-soup out there."

Lori looked back at Louis Paul. He held up his palm and tried to smile.

Blown from the car, barely feet from the roiling fireball, Knapp was acutely aware of everything. Flames still licked at the remainder of his shirt and pants. He pawed at them. Rolled away. Screaming. Leaving the burned clothes behind, burned into the asphalt. Searing pain, unbelievable pain devoured him. Screaming, screaming. He involuntarily clenched his fists. He soon realized he had no pain in his hands, and tried to focus on that single finding. His hands were covered with giant blisters and crusted blood. Fingers hidden, encapsulated in serum-filled balloons.

He tried to touch his face. He could see. Breathing was difficult. Nostrils, the boney parts, were charred, clotted with blood. His ears were roaring like a seashell, but he could hear. The last sounds he remembered were the screeching of brakes.

One of his trucks. One of his own trucks stopped. The truckers jumped from the cab and bolted for Mr. K. They saw a nude man, body contorted, limbs raw-beef-red, hands unidentifiable, face a mixture of blotched purple-red and charcoal pits. No eyelashes, brows, hair. Scalp, a mass of raw pulp. But...amazingly, half his body was untouched.

The lead driver, Todd Murphy, knew what to do. A gold crucifix hanging from his rearview mirror attested to his faith. Murphy had worked for Mr. K for years, driving insane hours and treacherous cargo in order to see his wife attain her nursing degree. He checked vital signs. Labored breathing. Racing heart.

The second driver only glanced at the scorched body. He immediately turned away and vomited.

"Get yourself together, partner. Damnit! Check around the vehicle. See if there's anyone else," snapped Murphy.

The sickened driver circled the burned-out car which still sparked with flames. He stopped abruptly, staring at the remains of a smoldering pile of a dismembered skeleton. "Murphy! Over here..."

The morning newspaper was next to a silver coffee pot on the dining table. Director Kelley read the headline: *Senator Joseph Trask of Illinois Found Dead in McLean.*

The lead article in the *Washington Post* stated, 'Death apparently was caused by a fall down the stairs leading to the basement.'

Kelley grunted, served himself scrambled eggs, chicken livers, and a dollop of grits from silver chafing dishes on the sideboard. A maid poured his coffee. Kelley stuck the starched white linen napkin in his collar and said to her, "Thank you, Mable. I'm famished."

The walk back to the pueblo took longer than usual; Louis Paul leaned on his son the last few miles. He wasn't hungry, telling his wife that he would rest, eat later. "Just some water," he said wearily.

Linda heard the glass hit the floor moments after she had placed it by the bed. She found him looking surprised and rubbing his neck. He apologized, and said, "He's dead."

"Who's dead? Not Doctor Bill..."

"No. The senator from Illinois. The man questioned me...Washington... my testimony. He ridiculed me."

38

Josh left the hospital, assured that Bill was in surgery.

Exhausted, Jack led Lori to the room where Bill would eventually be moved. They collapsed on the twin beds. Lori slept soundly, but Jack was tormented. Vivid, sickening nightmares.

Massive bear. A large hump on his back. Grizzly. Raging cavernous mouth. Red pupils. Roaring, screaming, rising to its full height and reaching out with deadly curved claws. Ripping, ripping, ripping. Fifteen-hundred pounds of muscle and fury. Blood-covered brown, white-tipped fur. Gabriel's blood. Blood everywhere. The event indelible in his mind.

Sweating, on fire, disoriented. Jack made it to the bathroom and threw up. He looked at himself in the mirror. It wasn't his reflection. Older. Long hair, scruffy beard. Sunburned. Dark sunken skin around bloodshot eyes. "I look like shit," he murmured. He couldn't even recognize his own voice when he hissed, "I hope that grizzly tore out his heart and ate it."

An hour later, Bill was moved into the room. Slanted rays of cool pale violet touched the rimrock. The windows of the U.S. Public Health Hospital in Gallup lit up. Early morning rounds. Lori scooted the only chair to the head of the bed. The screech was awful. Jack leaned against the deep windowsill, arms crossed, head down.

The floor charge nurse stepped into the room, saying, "Ms. Wilson, you have a phone call."

"May I take it in here?"

"Of course."

"Yolie here. Is it okay to talk?"

"I'm with Jack. What's going on?"

"The pot's gone from simmer to full boil. Your Chicago boss is in a piss-pot of trouble. Director Kelley is on his tail but good."

"What have they got on Brooks?"

"Seems someone has sent copies of a report detailing very illegal dealings at the Port Authority in Calumet. Sent to Kelley himself."

"Wonder who would be able to do that?"

Yolie cleared her throat. "*¿Pues?* I wonder. Who would ever want to burn SpecialagentinchargeassholeBrooks?"

"Does he suspect you?" Lori moved to the window, stretching the chord to the max.

"That's why I'm calling you, silly girl."

"How did you find me?"

"Lori, you've been so busy baby-sitting that Italian hunk of a doctor. It's a long story. For now, let's just say there's a forest ranger that is a really good guy, even with the limp. A colleague."

"I figured that out."

"Thought you would. Brooks screwed him good. Josh Flores is a very intuitive man—little gets past him. Brooks sent the poor guy on a risky assignment, his first crack out of the box. New to Montana, he got trapped by a booze-crazed tribal leader. A carbine round shattered the head of his femur. Joshua was treated locally, not sent to Denver. Good V.A. and Army hospitals there. Bad results, uncorrectable. Brooks dumped him. Listen, Lori, Director Kelley has called in experts from the Atomic Energy Commission. Any idea why?"

Lori repeated her question to Jack. "I think I know," he said. "Remember the Geiger counter going crazy? When we got in the Wagoneer? Let me talk to her."

"Hey, Yolanda. It's Jack D'Amico. Thanks for watching over Agent Wilson who's watching over me."

"Any time, Doctor. So why the AEC? Why would the director of the FBI bring them into the picture?"

"Yellowcake. They were burying big blue barrels of it at the Salt Lake. No one would notice or question the new radiation."

Lori reached for the phone. "Yolie, what was Senator Trask up to?"

"Later. I'm in Albuquerque."

"What?"

"I quit. Josh met me. He's getting my luggage." As a parting zinger, she added, "I'm a free *Chicana* and I'm going to kick ass. See you for breakfast."

Lori turned to Jack. "She's fearless. I'll bet you she's dug up lots of intel. Nothing in Washington is really hidden—it's all glass. She could get hurt."

"The only way to kill a story is to have some dead people. That's exactly what happened to my family," Jack said, gritting his teeth.

Louis Paul sat in a rocker. Tito sat cross-legged in front of him. "The evil is not gone. I feel its presence, near." His tone of voice resonated with sadness, heartbreak. "Our senator, Richard Phillips, is at his ranch. I watched through his window. Telephone call made him very upset."

"Do you know why?"

"No. Cowboy saw me. I ran to Box Canyon."

"Phillips—the white man that made a fool of you in Washington?"

"Yes."

"You're going after him, aren't you?"

⬦ ⬦ ⬦

Taos. The ranch house. Phillips was once a big man, now he was wizened, hunched. He drained the last swallow of coffee, wiped his thin lips. Dropped the *Journal* to the wood floor.

Trask's death was big news. Network headliners reported on the senator's work, legislation, words of regret from his colleagues.

Using two canes, he pulled himself out of the chair. He cursed the wet weather, the long flight from DC, the chill of the hacienda, no sleep. It all combined to make a perfect storm, wracking his limbs with constant pain. He moved slowly to his drawing table, nearly slipping on a Navajo rug. He snapped on a gooseneck lamp and swiveled to a long oak map cabinet adjacent to his desk. Long narrow drawers. Meticulous museum-quality preservation sheets. He flipped the sheets until he found the one he wanted.

New Mexico. Arizona. Red lines marked the Zuni reservation boundaries. Green delineated the sacred Salt Lake. Purple identified mining sites. Blue areas marked...

A knock on the door interrupted him. "Yes?"

"Sir, seen a bear this morning—early." It was Ray, Phillip's foreman. Rain dribbled on to the floor from his yellow slicker. He pulled out a red bandana to mop his face and hat. He was as old as the senator, and totally dedicated to him.

"Where?"

"Box Canyon."

"That's too close. Kill it." Phillips paused, looking at the foreman's expressionless face. "After you get him, come have lunch with me. Maria's making red enchiladas."

"Yes, sir."

Phillips gazed down at the blue areas—water sources. Water Sources.

His constituents with deep pockets and mineral leases. Trask wanting federal boundaries re-aligned had seemed innocuous at the time. He had listened to NPR earlier in the morning—the only decent source of national news in the hick state. A single sentence made him choke on a swallow of coffee.

Before Trask's death, the FBI had been investigating the senator and his involvement with a uranium mine in Canada.

His boney finger flipped to a tab in a worn leather journal. He fumbled, finally managed to dial the number. A terse 'Yes'. Unfamiliar voice.

"Is Mr. Knapp available?"

"He's dead." The line clicked and all he heard was a very loud dial tone.

Phillips was alone. Suddenly irritable. Trask had abandoned him. Then suddenly elated, he was the sole survivor. The recipient of all the future money.

Louis Paul washed his long hair in *amole* suds. Brushed it until it shone. The silver white streak came alive.

Holding the ancient fetish in his palm, he allowed himself to rise to a different level. At peace. Real. His world came into stronger focus. The sky was bluer.

When he was young, only six or seven winters, his father had taught him that all land, rivers, streams, all real powers of Nature, privately owned or not, belong to our land. Ancestral land.

They came. Took our lands. Herded us into their imposed corrals like cattle. Left us barren land. Dry rivers. Poisoned water.

He lowered his head in shame, speaking softly. "Mother Earth, insulted. They absorb and destroy Salt Lake, Sacred Mother." The fetish warmed in his hands. He rubbed it. Almost dropped it. The lifeline of the bear was glowing red.

Fetish in his pocket. At the single window he looked out upon *Dowa Yalanne.*

Aloud, he said to the sacred mountain, "I am ready to leave my body."

Eggs over easy, green chile sausage, biscuits. Coffee. Lori smiled at Jack over the thick lip of her mug. "Glad your appetite is back."

Mouth full, Jack asked, "Heard from Yolie yet?"

She started to speak when she saw a man step into the diner. "Josh!"

"Room for two more?" he responded.

"*Pues*, I certainly hope so," said a woman behind him. "Look what the red-eye flight brought in." Low-slung bell bottom jeans held up with a neon tie-dyed scarf. White poet's shirt tied at the midriff. Large silver loop earrings and a smile as big as Colorado. Yolie was in fine form.

"I'm retired! No more Brooks. No more Chicago. No more crap raining down from Washington." Her OJ arrived. A vodka miniature appeared out of a huge purse.

After a long drink from the screwdriver, she told them Senator Phillips had sponsored the bill dealing with the boundaries at Salt Lake. The bastard was back in New Mexico, at his ranch above Taos. "One of our agents answered the phone in Knapp's office; it was Phillips."

"What were our guys after?" asked Lori.

"Bills of lading. Bills of lading containing Canadian uranium-rich ore." As though thinking out loud, she added, "Knapp dead. Trask dead. Only Phillips is alive."

Jack sat back in the booth, saying, "Let's go get the bastard. Let him explain whatthefuck they were up to."

Lori took over. "We eat, get organized. Josh, set us up with everything you've got."

His strength ebbing, Louis Paul, a bag tied to his belt, climbed slowly down the creaky ladder exiting his home in the pueblo. The day was not good. Bad things will happen. He touched the bear fetish in his pocket.

He walked quietly through the semi-dark vacant passageways, softly saying his prayers. Dogs. Mongrels. Grey, sandy, mixed-color coats. Joined him. Occasional whimpers, no barking. He emerged from the pueblo complex, crossed the parking area in front of the mission. Without a signal, the pack of dogs jumped into the bed of his pickup.

Louis Paul drove north-east. Albuquerque. Santa Fe. Espanola. Velarde. When he passed the church in Ranchos de Taos, the early sun cast long, deep shadows. The familiar drive reminded him of his first summons to the Phillips ranch. The denigrating diatribe he had endured there. All a loss.

He saw the entrance, drove past, and forced the truck down a riddled dry arroyo, pock-marked with boulders. When he gunned the truck out of the sandy bottom, he topped out on a ridge where he could survey Box Canyon. With a simple hand tap on his leg, the dogs quickly were at his side. Several whimpered. Others wagged their tails. He removed the pouch from his belt and passed small grease cakes to each dog. They will need this, he thought.

With a sweeping motion, the dogs understood. Each found shelter in a clump of sagebrush or rock cluster, their coats dictating the choice of camouflage. Now out of sight to the casual observer, the dogs lay awaiting new instruction.

Jack saw him first. Lori pulled off 66, reversed. Tito hopped in the back seat of the Wagoneer.

"Hey, man, where're you headed?" asked Jack.

"North," Tito responded.

"You normally hitchhike when you're going—I believe you said, north?" asked Lori.

"Father took the truck. I know where he's going. He will need my help."

"Why?" asked Jack.

"Have you heard of Senator Phillips?" said Tito.

They joined up at Josh's home. Tito remained in the Wagoneer.

Before Josh raided the vault stocked with weapons and ammunition, he had covered the large windows facing the drive-in lanes with newspaper. Lori complimented his choice of wallpaper.

Josh pushed his dark glasses back on his thick hair. "Love the mellow light. Pretty clever for a defunct FBI agent."

"You will always be an agent," Yolanda said. "You weren't fired. Your career was ambushed."

"Thank you for the clarification," said Josh.

Lori pulled on a FBI vest, then thrust a pair to Jack and Josh. "Josh Flores is hereby reinstated, and Doctor D'Amico has been deputized and will serve as Special Medical Agent. Agent Cervantes, will you second my motion?"

"I second Agent Wilson's motion," said Yolie.

"Let's roll," said Lori. "We have another man to deputize. Louis Paul's son, Tito. She tossed a duffle bag to him, who added it to the pile in the Wagoneer. Josh took the wheel. Lori sat shotgun, a Remington .30-06 with a bore-sighted riflescope by her side. Vest pockets laden with rounds of steeltip ammo.

In the back seat, Jack loaded a Beretta 9MM handgun. Yolie preferred a Glock. She gave her handgun an affectionate pat, leaned against Jack's shoulder, promptly fell asleep. He nodded off moments later. His life now seemed to have purpose.

Tito remained alert, focused. Silent.

Phillips hung up—more calls from news media. A television on a rolling cart spewed sound bytes. *Corruption. Uranium. Enriched uranium ore shipped to the Southwest.* His name wasn't mentioned...yet.

He knew details of his realignment bill would soon hit the fan. He called his Albuquerque office, told them to set up a press conference for late afternoon.

39

*M*urphy had watched his wife in action in the ER. He knew something about burn victims. After cleaning Knapp's wounds as best as he could with hydrogen peroxide, he had applied Vaseline, encasing the worst areas in plastic wrap. He prayed the poor, unconscious man wouldn't wake up until they found help.

The semi belched and began rolling. At the wheel, Murphy reached for the CB microphone.

"Who're you calling? We're not scheduled to report for another two hours."

"Control."

Knapp's second-in-command instructed them to take the boss to Senator Phillips' ranch. Explicit directions. No hospital, the boss wouldn't want that. As a second thought, the man asked, "How bad is he?"

"Real bad. Half his face. Half his torso," said Murphy. "He could die on us any minute. If I wasn't a religious guy, I'd leave him."

Knapp Chemical Processing Company's main office was in chaos. FBI agents were all over the place. A driver team reported that Knapp was near death. Washington was notified.

Maria cleared the table, balancing beer glasses and a near-empty plate of *bizcochos*. *"Muchas gracias, Maria,"* said Phillips. "Ray, come with me."

The senator slowly made it to his desk. Lit a cigarette. Offered one to Ray, saying, "I'm calling a press conference for late this afternoon. No more crap is going to come out of those shitty press guys, catch my drift? Slick pricks with their lies. Lies!" He slammed both hands on the table. "Only the jackass from KOB, and that guy from the <u>Albuquerque Journal.</u> But you search them, and their staff. Don't you dare let anyone you haven't checked get to the house." Ray started for the door, but was interrupted.

"Get the men. Pull them off whatever they're doing. Spread them high and low. Tell them to shoot anything you point to."

"You got it, sir." Ray left, the unlit cigarette in the corner of his mouth.

Thunder reverberated across the chamisa-covered plains below Taos. Wheeler Peak was shrouded by cumulonimbus clouds, towering vertically. Rain on the way.

"Watch for 64 going to Eagle Nest," Jack said from the back seat. Map in hand, he added, "The turn-off is after the church in Ranchos de Taos."

The winding road climbed and narrowed, in and out of pale light. Tight turns, flowing water to the right, crossing to the left. Granite spikes. The sky darkened. A battered pickup ahead slowed them down, then began to drift to the other lane.

"Looks like that dude is hammered," Josh said.

"Peel out when you can. Something in my bones says we better get moving," snapped Lori.

"Right on." Looking in the rearview mirror, Josh saw Yolie hand a file folder to Jack. "Wait 'til you see what she's got on him, Jack."

"I've nailed him. Copies have been mailed to Director Kelley. I intend to wrap this up," Yolie said, peeling an orange. She handed a segment to Jack. "Doctor Jack, any special woman in your life?"

Jack popped the orange in his mouth, rolled down the window a bit. Spit out a seed. "No time. I'll do it right later."

Lori smiled, but he didn't see it.

The gate was open, easily spotted. The landmark, an open yoke with *PHILLIPS RANCH* clearly carved into the wood. The sidelifter turned on to the rutted dirt road. Only minutes passed before a white, mud-splattered pickup drove straight at them. Both trucks stopped.

A stooped elderly guy wearing a slicker, rifle barrel partially revealed, climbed from his vehicle. He called out, "What do you guys want? Are you lost?"

Murphy looked down from the cab at the man. "We've got a critical burn victim." Windshield wipers scraped the glass. "We were told to bring him here. The senator's a real good friend of my boss."

"I'll be the judge of that," Ray said. "Well, you can't turn around here. Too tight for your rig. Follow me up to the house. The senator can check out your story."

"What about the patient?" Murphy said.

"Get him out. The boss will want to see him. If need be, we can put him in the bunkhouse." Ray kicked his muddy boots against the running board. Backed the truck up the drive, went inside to get the senator.

The drivers had placed Knapp on a clean white sheet in the sleeping compartment. Luckily, the man was out cold. Murphy told the other driver to crouch behind Knapp's head, so he could slowly pull the sheet forward until they could lift the sheet and lower him to the ground.

Phillips and the foreman watched from the front porch. Knapp's clubfoot touched the ground. His mouth opened. Only a garbled moan. One eye opened.

Despite the hideous devastation, Phillips recognized Knapp. "Shoot him! Shoot all of them," snapped the senator.

Ray raised his rifle and did what he was told.

Unexpectedly, Phillips attacked Ray from behind with full force, knocking him to the ground. The rifle skidded away in the gravel drive. Using his cane, Phillips repeatedly struck him on the head, then ripped off Ray's yellow slicker, and grabbed the rifle.

Stunned, shaking his head, and spitting out gravel, Ray managed to turn to see the senator running away without his canes, waving the rifle.

"Should be there soon," said Jack, speaking loudly over the roar of the Wagoneer. "We should hit a broad plain, the lake at Eagle Nest. It's just beyond that, on the left."

"I want to make something clear," said Lori. "I'm the youngest, but I'm in charge. I'll also take the blame if we screw up. As a federal agent, I outrank Josh. Yolie's been behind a desk too long. Jack and Tito are civvies. I'm also an expert shot."

"I'm okay with that," said Jack.

In unison, the rest of the team agreed. Lori was the boss.

"This is the goddamned windiest road I've ever seen," said Jack. "There it is. Turn left. Right there." Josh hit the brakes, swerved off 64 and on to the dirt road.

"Thanks for the advance notice," said Josh.

At last, Tito spoke. "I have been here before. I was very young, but I remember a big, fancy house. Not far, surrounded by hills. We should..."

"Stay high," finished Lori.

Josh downshifted, engaged the four-wheel drive. "Which way, kid?"

Tito closed his eyes. "Right. I feel it."

Within minutes of leaving the road, they topped out on a rugged hill. The hacienda was directly below. Lori was instantly out, standing on the running board.

"What the hell?" muttered Jack. A sidelifter—a huge semi-trailer—and a pickup were parked in the circular drive. There were lifeless bodies sprawled on the ground. Front door wide open. A woman appeared momentarily at the door, then disappeared.

"We walk from here," said Lori. "Lock and load. Tito, you stay put. Watch for anyone else approaching. Josh, you lead. I'll cover your backs."

Moving low and fast, Josh reached the semi. Protected from view, he inched toward the bodies. Jack placed a hand on his shoulder. Josh jerked back, whispering, "Stay back, Doc."

Jack ignored him. Moved forward to examine the victims. Yolie and Lori moved quickly to the porch. With no coaxing, Maria stepped outside. Hands up. Tears running down her cheeks.

"¿Donde esta el senador?" asked Yolie. Maria stared at her blankly, wondering whether to tell her where he went. "Señora, por favor, es muy importante." She held up her shield. "¿Entiende?"

"La carretera que atra viesa el cañón," said Maria.

"Tenemos que salir. Quidate." Yolie turned to leave.

Maria reached out to touch her arm. "Vaya con Dios."

Outside, two of the bodies had bullet holes in their heads. Killed instantly. The third. Partially charred face. Partially burned body. Jack guessed fifty percent. He rolled him over. Even with half a face burned beyond recognition, he still recognized him.

"Knapp. Anthony Knapp." He called out for Lori. "You were right. It's Mr. K, the sonofabitch that had my family murdered!"

"No time to celebrate, team," said Lori. She spun around to see Tito. "I told you to stay with the Jeep. The weapons..."

"Jeep is behind the barn. Somehow I knew where to go. I spotted eight men. With rifles. Guarding a ridge above Box Canyon."

"Maria said there was a little-used trail that would lead to Cañón de Cajón," said Yolie.

Lori took over. "Tito, get the Jeep. Josh, Jack, move the bodies. Cover them up. Yolie, make sure Maria is safe. I'm calling this in."

"Slower, Josh," Lori said.

Hunkered behind the wheel, Josh crept along the steep track leading into the box canyon, watching the armed men. Spaced at one-hundred yard in a semi-circle around the rim above them. None of the riflemen had made a move. Time seemed to no longer exist. There was no time at all. Only the Now.

The thousand-foot cliff creating the end of the canyon came into view as they slowly rounded a bend. The canyon floor, dotted with chamisa, scrub pine, narrowed. Closing in on them. The Jeep entered deep shadows. Josh pulled to a stop, and asked, "What are the rifle boys doing?"

"Nothing," said Jack and Yolie in unison.

"Well, no better time than now," said Lori. She opened her door and climbed out, keeping both hands in full view. A breeze ruffled her hair. She raised her arms, turned around. The yellow FBI insignia on her vest obvious. One by one, the others climbed out.

Tito, the last one out, was the first to notice. The riflemen had disappeared. They all heard the sounds of baying dogs ricocheting off the canyon walls.

"What just happened?" said Jack.

"I have no idea," responded Tito.

In the shadows, Phillips crouched between two massive boulders abutting the canyon wall. *I'm cornered.* He pushed harder against the cliff face. Wild-eyed, he fired the rifle haphazardly. Shots reverberated back and forth, making it impossible to determine their origin.

"Everyone down," yelled Lori. "Spread out."

Phillips kept firing until the magazine was empty. He dropped the rifle, lowered his head, closed his eyes. "Come get me," he mumbled out loud. A huge bear rose upright one hundred feet away. The grizzly moved toward him. A roar. Another vicious, terrifying, threatening roar.

"Father!" screamed Tito. He ran toward the grizzly.

Another enormous menacing roar filled the air. The entire canyon. Before their eyes, the bear dropped to all fours, loped amazingly fast down the backside of the hill and out of sight.

"Father!" Tito stopped abruptly, dropped to his knees.

They caught up with Tito. They all saw what remained of a mutilated body.

Jack ignored the bloody mass, his focus on Tito. Tito's face contorted, a deep, pitiful groan rolled forth between clinched teeth. He tipped over to the ground, writhing in overwhelming pain. Jack dropped down beside him. Lori, too. Tito's body twitched involuntarily.

Lori tapped Jack on his shoulder. "Look."

Twenty feet behind them, the dogs were sitting down, all silently looking at Tito. A cold blast of air poured over the mountain peaks, sweeping down into the canyon. Lenticular clouds condensed in the crest of the waves. A split second after the sun dropped below the horizon, the polished pearl-like clouds diffracted. A flash.

A high-pitched, unearthly scream emitted from above. Looking up, Jack saw a huge bird diving straight at him. Not at Jack. Straight for Tito.

"Lori! Falcon," whispered Jack. They both ducked. Hit the dirt, his body protecting her.

Another ear-piercing sound enveloped them, like the bugle of a monster bull elk. The charged air churned around them. The peregrine falcon's wings whipped viciously as it whirled past, accelerating skyward. At lightning speed, the outline of the bird quickly turned to a tiny black dot. Gone.

Tito fainted.

"What's happening?" Jack said aloud. Tito?" Jack looked at him intently. "Breathe. Breathe, Tito."

Tears flooded Tito's cheeks. He opened his eyes. "Father is dead."

Lori noticed the fetish in Tito's hand. A small bear. "Where did you get..."

"Father passed it to me."

"When?"

"As his Spirit passed."

The End

Author's Notes

Dr. Jacobs lived and worked at the Black Rock Hospital, Zuni Pueblo. Adding to his experiences, the author found the following sources invaluable:

Zuni Folk Tales, Frank Hamilton Cushing, G. P. Putnam's Sons, 1901. First edition.

My Adventures in Zuñi, Frank Hamilton Cushing, with additions to the original volume by Cushing and E. DeGolyer, plus *An Aboriginal Pilgrimage* by Sylvester Baxter, The Peripatetic Press, Santa Fe, NM, 1941.

The Zuni Enigma, Nancy Yaw Davis, W. W. Norton & Co.

A Zuni Life, Virgil Wyaco, University of New Mexico Press, 1998.

Zuni and the American Imagination, Eliza McFeely, Hill & Wang, 2001.

Zuni Fetishes, Frank Hamilton Cushing, K C Publications, Forth Printing, 1972.

A Guide to Zuni Fetishes and Carvings, Kent McManus, Treasure Chest Books.

Salt Lake: The Beautiful and the Dangerous, Barbara Tedlock, University of New Mexico Press, 1992.

A Matter of Genocide, Ward Churchill, City Lights Books, San Francisco, 1997.

The Hand Book of Pharmacy & Theraputics, Eli Lilly Co., 1927.

Medicinal Plants of the Mountain West, Michael Moore, Museum of New Mexico Press, 1987.

Traditional Zuni Food, Rita Edaakie, A:shiwi A:wan Museum and Heritage Center, 1999.

Pueblo Indian Cookbook, Phyllis Hughes, Museum of New Mexico Press, 1979.

The Peregrine, J. A. Baker, HarperCollins Publishers Ltd., London, 1967.

Zuni Stew was edited by Sallie Ritter.

Readers Guide

1. After testifying before Congress, Bill is still enraged by the uranium poisoning aided by the Small Business Administration. Did that open your eyes to the birth defects, cancer, loss of livestock and lives among the Pueblos of New Mexico?
2. How did the relationship between Jack and Lori change?
3. Senators Trask and Phillips are behind the plot to move the boundaries at Sacred Lake. Did their mastery of corruption ring true?
4. As an educated man, how does Jack interpret the paranormal? For example, the resurrection of Christ can be seen as mythology. Even though something cannot be explained, can it still be true?
5. Bill is happy with his life on the Zuni reservation even though he lost his first love. Did you feel his *"simpatico"* with the Zunis?
6. Lori is thought of as a naïve rookie by Agent Brooks. When did she figure out that Brooks was crooked, and who had the proof?
7. Yolie holds her head high, the epitome of a feminist *Chicana*. Did she ring true?
8. Tito tells Jack that there is no time in Zuni. Do you understand the differences between their divergent worlds?
9. Will Tito carry on as a *shiwani*?
10. Josh was mistreated by the government, left with an irreparable injury. Yet he is surprisingly intuitive. Were you impressed with his forethought?
11. Historically the Catholic Church attempted to destroy the indigenous religions. Were you aware of the conflicting worlds, the history of crimes against the Native Americans?
12. The physical beauty of New Mexico becomes a character unto itself. Did the people, the landscape and culture of New Mexico come alive, and were you able to enter that world?
13. Cosmology, the supernatural, and magic are constant themes in the novel. Have you ever been confronted with such events?
14. Symbols, such as a fetish, have a "presence" in Louis Paul's world. Animals, such as the peregrine falcon, guide and/or protect. Was this convincing?

15. Zunis believe Nature to be the guiding force of all things. For instance, they believe even a pebble has a soul. How does Nature influence your life?
16. Light is a constant theme, especially a mirage, as in the astonishing scene with Jack and Bill in the Piper. Did this phenomenon seem real to you? Have you ever experienced bending light?
17. Is *Zuni Stew* a murder mystery, a romance or what?
18. Give examples of the voice, the details used to emulate 1973, such as Route 66, Haight Ashbury, Watergate.
19. The slaughter of the D'Amico family was ordered by Anthony Knapp, and carried out by Gabriel. Was there resolution?
20. Jack feels his anguish, remorse disappear, to be replaced with calm after eating Zuni stew. If any reader should want to try it, the recipe follows.

Recipe for Zuni Stew

White Corn Hominy:

1 quart dry white corn kernels
2 quarts water
1/2 cup slacked lime (available at builders supply firms)

Dissolve lime in water in large kettle. Add corn and stir well. Boil for 30 minutes or until hulls loosen. Let stand 30 minutes then wash thoroughly in cold water, working with hands until dark tips of kernels are removed. Rinse again until water is clear. (Always used for posoli.)

Stew:

2 cups posoli corn (lime hominy)
6 cups water
1 lb. pigs feet, beef tripe, cubed pork or lamb, or 2 1/2 lbs. pork ribs
1/2 pork rind
4 red chile pods made into unseasoned sauce or 3 tablespoons red chile powder
1 tablespoon chopped onion
2 teaspoons salt
2 teaspoons oregano

Cook posoli corn in water to cover until kernels pop. Add red chile sauce or powder, meat and pork rind. Bring to boil in covered kettle, adding water to cover as needed and simmer until meat is well cooked and corn is tender, at least four hours at low temperature. Day long cooking at lowest simmer temperature improves flavor even more. Cut meat from bones and add chopped onion and seasoning. (Green chiles, roasted and chopped may be substituted for red.) Simmer covered an additional thirty minutes.

Serves four to six.

◈From *Pueblo Indian Cookbook*, compiled and edited by Phyllis Hughes, Museum of New Mexico Press, Santa Fe, NM, 1972.

CPSIA information can be obtained
at www.ICGtesting.com
Printed in the USA
FSOW01n0716060215
5057FS